Treacherous LOVE

Treacherous LOVE

THE DIARY OF AN ANONYMOUS TEENAGER

Edited by
Beatrice Sparks, Ph.D.

AVON BOOKS

An Imprint of HarperCollinsPublishers

Library of Congress Catalog Card Number: 99-96355
ISBN: 0-380-80862-5
❖
First Avon Books edition, 2000

AVON TRADEMARK REG. U.S. PAT. OFF. AND IN OTHER COUNTRIES,
MARCA REGISTRADA, HECHO EN U.S.A.

DEDICATED
To all kids, everywhere.

WHAT YOU *DON'T KNOW CAN* HURT YOU!
Roger Young, an FBI agent says, "The biggest mistake
people can make is to think that *it* just doesn't happen
here, that we're safe. The size of the town doesn't
matter—sexual exploitation of children
occurs everywhere."

Treacherous LOVE

September 9th—Monday—1:15 a.m.

I just woke up with a cold spooky feeling running through me. At first I couldn't figure out what it was and pulled myself deeper under my covers and put my pillow over my head, but the shivers just got worse . . . then I realized Mom and Dad were fighting *again*! I HATE IT . . . HATE IT . . . HATE IT . . . when they do that!

I can't understand a single bit of what they are saying, but the feelings come through like giant rocks and electric shocks and fire darts. I want it to stop!!! Stop!!! Stop!!! I hate it! And I *hate them for doing it*! I don't really hate them. Actually, I want, with all my might, to run into their room and snuggle up in their bed with them. Me in the middle being kissed and hugged and spoiled like when I was little.

Whatever happened to our loving, happy little family that used to play hide-and-seek in the house and have picnics on the floor in front of the fireplace on rainy days? And do all the fun nice things that we always used to do? Like talk and talk and talk and talk.

MONDAY—7:00 A.M.

My stupid old alarm clock just woke me up with its stupid old song, "Oh, What a Beautiful Morning." It's hardly that! My pillow is all wet and soggy with tears and I'm as tired as if I had just climbed Mount Everest. I guess I cried myself to sleep again last night. I hate that!

MONDAY—7:36 A.M.

I just got out of the shower and finished drying my hair and *I AM SO EMBARRASSED*! How could I have felt all those horrible hating things about Mom and Dad last night?

As the warm bubbly water splashed and gurgled over my body it washed all the badness away and made me think more like a sane person instead of like a dumb little kid. *They* have a right to disagree about things just like I do! They aren't clones. They don't have to just say "yes sir" or "yes ma'am" to each other to death about every little thing. Bridget and I sometimes have almost screaming matches over who played the best at some of our hockey games and other stuff that's not all that important, so why couldn't Mom and Dad have just been arguing about a movie they'd seen or Mom's alcoholic sister Meg, who comes by occasionally and drives us all crazy, or . . . there are a million things . . . oh, I'm such a worrywart, look-for-trouble, negative, dumbhead sometimes.

8:14 A.M.

I'm ready to take off for breakfast and school . . . *BUT* I've still got a tiny uneasy little feeling in the pit of my stomach. Ummmm, I *know* Mom and Dad were just having a friendly little blow-off like Bridget and I do! It's got to be that. It's really, truly, got to be a stupid little blow-off.

September 11th—Wednesday—10:00 p.m.

I got 92 percent on my math test today. Kyoto and I were the only two in our whole class who got over 77. I tried to pretend it was nothing, but inside I'm carbonating, bubbling, popping, and hopping in every single solitary white and red blood cell in my body.

It was a state test to see how we stack up against . . . I don't know who . . . and it was hard as anything. Actually, I had to guess at a few of the questions, but at least I guessed right, and *I have been studying* like an obsessed person.

I'm glad I'm good in math, because I'm a dummy on all my other subjects. Well, maybe not really a dummy but not really good. Dad keeps telling me I've got to have more confidence in myself.

How I wish I could talk to him like I used to even a few months ago. I really want to share my bubbly feeling with someone. I've got to! Before the cork pops out of the top of my head and my brains go spewing all over the ceiling. He had a late meeting and ate dinner at his office.

11:20 P.M.

I couldn't sleep so I went into the family room to watch TV. Dad's paper was lying in his lap but he wasn't reading. He felt me standing there and reached up, grabbed my hand and pulled me down on his lap. I felt his tears drip on my cheek and whispered, "What's wrong, Daddy, please tell me what's wrong."

"Nothing, baby," he said wetly. "I'm just not feeling too well these days."

The bubbles all popped in my body and mind, and my heart exploded in my throat. How selfish I'd been to be thinking only of myself. Words and thoughts erupted out of my mouth, though I tried to keep them back. "Do you have . . . cancer? Are you going to . . . you know . . . ?"

Daddy hugged me so tightly I could barely breathe. It made me feel safe and comfortable and *important,* yet scared and angry at the same time.

Then he patted my cheek gently. "I think your mom and I both have some kind of . . . horrible something that seems to be infecting most of the adult world these days," he said.

"Is it . . . ?" I couldn't bear to use the word *terminal. It* seemed so TERMINAL!

Daddy sensed my morbid feelings and the slightest hint of a laugh squeaked out of him. "Oh, baby. Honest, it's nothing big. It's more inconvenient and annoying than anything else." He stopped for a second. "Mom and I will get better. We'll help each other. I PROMISE!" He kissed my cheek and sent me off to bed. Part of me was happy and part of me was sad. I can't explain.

It's sort of like those candies that are really sweet but sour, too, only a THOUSAND, MILLION, ZILLION TIMES HEAVIER.

Why did I write "heavier"? Feelings aren't heavy, or are they? Sometimes they're heavier than anything else, even though you can't see them or hold them. It's confusing! I wonder if I'm the only one in the whole wide world and the galaxies outside the world who's trampled and trapped and confused by crazy, maybe nothing, things.

September 12th—Thursday—4:10 p.m.

Mrs. Marress honored me and Kyoto in front of the class by giving each of us a little banner. It was embarrassing and my face must have been as red as Kyoto's. I'm sure *everyone* in the class thought it was stupid!

I *want* to show the banner to Mom and Dad, but I don't, too. It's a silly dumb feeling and *I'd just be trying to show off.*

4:29 P.M.

I found a note Mom had left on the refrigerator door saying she and Dad were taking the afternoon off and going up to Lake Happy Reflection, and they probably wouldn't be home until late. I wonder what that's all about. Come to think about it, Lake Happy Reflection would be a *great* place to go when you're feeling sick, or even just head or heart sick. I hope they're remembering the wonderful times we used to have there when I was little, and we'd take picnics and build sand castles and play endless, silly, pretend games. I hope! Hope! Hope! *That's* what they're doing.

11:18 P.M.

It's almost midnight and Mom and Dad aren't home yet. Tomorrow's a workday and they hardly ever stay up late on workdays.

11:27 P.M.

I wonder if they've been in an accident or something. The winding road coming down from the lake has a lot of sharp turns on it. It would be really easy to skid off the side and go careening down . . . down . . . down. Now I'm hallucinating like Aunt Meg at her very worst, when she's been drinking. Mom and Dad are probably sitting out on the beach digging their bare toes into the sand and watching the moon's reflection bouncing up and down on the tiny waves in the water. Oh, how I wish I were with them. Why didn't they take me? That's easy. They didn't want me with them!!! Why would they want sourpuss me when they're both feeling so unhappy? I *know* they're unhappy because they both work late and when they're together it's like they're playing the "don't touch me" avoidance game with each other.

I *don't want* to think of negative things anymore! I JUST WANT THEM TO COME HOME. I don't want to see their splattered bodies in my head, lying on the rocks off the side of the road. It's too gruesome and stupid, but it won't go away.

I guess I'll go crash on the couch in the family room so I can hear them when they come in. I *KNOW* they'll come in soon . . . Please, Mom and Dad, please come in soon!

September 13th—Friday—6:21 a.m.

I can sweetly remember, sometime in the night, Mom and Dad putting me, a teenager, to bed. It was so wonderful and warm and everything a family should be! I can still hear them giggling softly as they tucked me in and kissed me, then tiptoed off to bed themselves. This is the way families should be. And the way our family is always *going to be from now on!*

8:49 P.M.

Our girls hockey team won 4 to 1. It was so awesome I feel like I'm barely tied down to earth. Something about elation and winning seems to defy gravity. Isn't life strange and wonderful and beautiful?

Mom and Dad were both there, and I played my heart out for them because they weren't killed coming home last night. Oh, yes, and because Chad Greer told me how "awesome" I was before the game. He even said he wished I was on the boys team. That's about enough to blow my mind out of orbit. He is so, so, so, so, SO yummy! Every girl at school has him on her wish list. Including me! I wish I had a magic lamp, then I'd have it made! All my wishes would come true! How's that for covering everything?

September 14th—Saturday—3:20 p.m.

Today as Bridget and I were coming home from the mall, and after we'd talked about boys—and Chad!—forever, I told her about my horrible night thinking about Mom and Dad running off the road, and how SCARY REAL all the horrible thoughts seemed, and how they went on and on with the goriest of details. I even told her about my stupid feelings that maybe they didn't love each other anymore. We sat on

a bench in front of Mr. Potter's flower shop. A funny
sign on his door said CLOSED GONE FISHING so nobody
came by.

I'm amazed at how good talking to Bridget made
me feel. It was really lovely, like I was pouring out all
my problems and she was *helping me help them*
evaporate into nothingness. I told her how horrible it
was to think that if Mom and Dad had died my nutty
alcoholic Aunt Meg might have taken over. What a life
that would be! I had never mentioned Aunt Meg to
anyone before. I guess because I'm ashamed and
embarrassed by her. She's married to nice Uncle
Harry, and he's wealthy as can be and she's got
everything money can buy and she's as beautiful as a
movie star but . . . she's still a drunk. Bridget and I
can't figure out *why*! Nobody can!

Bridget said she has a cousin Robert, two years
older than she, who was in a car accident that left him
"almost a vegetable." She said she never talked about
him either. She shrugged. It was okay because I could
see him in my mind.

"Poor, poor Robert," I said. "How dreadfully sad
that he can't talk or run or go to school and do all the
things we can." Then I hung my head because of how
unappreciative I have always been about my blessings
in life.

Bridget and I walked over to the park, and after we
had found a quiet private place we talked some more
about how lucky we were. We started naming little
things like eyes, nose, fingers, toes, and could have
gone on forever except we knew our moms would be
worried if we didn't come home.

I think *this* has been one of the nicest days in my
life! Isn't that strange, and it all started when Bridget

and I changed our negative thinking about Meg and Robert to . . . I guess . . . compassion. I know Aunt Meg hates what she does and is, and Robert can't help his situation.

Bridget and I are going to start writing down at least three wonderful things we're grateful for EVERY DAY. Oprah does that. I could write a whole diary full *every day* if I had the time and space.

---

1. I'M SOOOOO GRATEFUL FOR MY PRECIOUS MOM AND DAD, EVEN IF THEY DO BUG ME SOMETIMES. (ACTUALLY, I REALLY *APPRECIATE* THEIR BUGGING! I KNOW THEY'RE TRYING TO HELP ME.)

2. I'M SOOOO GRATEFUL FOR SCHOOL, WHERE I CAN GET AN EDUCATION. (EVEN IF IT'S SOMETIMES SO BORING I WANT TO DIE.)

3. I'M SOOOO GRATEFUL FOR THE IVY VINE THAT HAS CRAWLED UP THE WALL AND WHOSE TWISTED LITTLE FOLDED-UP LEAVES ARE CREEPING RIGHT *INSIDE* MY WINDOW. I HOPE MOM WILL LET THEM CLIMB ALL OVER MY ROOM.

I love Bridget! I really truly deeply do! I can talk to her about anything, anything in the whole wide world! How blessed I am to have a friend like her. I will cherish her always, through eternities and infinity! Thanks, thanks, thanks dear, kind, wise, loving, caring friend. Now, if Chad would pay a little more attention to me I'd contentedly float right off the planet. It's like he likes me but he's afraid of me. That doesn't make sense but it's how it seems. Maybe he's just shy and immature. That's what Bridget thinks.

September 15th—Sunday—6:31 p.m.

Mom had a bunch of her nerdy co-workers over for lunch. All they could talk about was how to choose mutual funds, putting together the right portfolio, do stock fund investors charge too much, etc., etc., etc., boring, boring, boring, and I had to sit there and pretend to be listening and interested. HARD JOB! It's the only time in my life I *couldn't wait* to get up and do the dishes.

7:02 P.M.

Bridget came over for an hour. Thank goodness! I *had* to be refueled with worthwhile reality stuff like boys, boys, boys, and clothes, clothes, clothes. Oh, yes, and hockey. We're playing Mountain Crest Middle School on Saturday and we've got to beat the socks off them and we will! Maybe then some of the guys will look at us like we aren't dirt clods. It seems like now only the nerds give me a second look, and only the scumballs hit on Bridget. That's probably because she's got big boobs. I wish I had big boobs— or any boobs at all. I look like I've got two fried eggs on my chest. "Woe is me." I saw that in an old silent movie. I love it! Woe is me.

Oops . . . erase. I forgot I was "going for the gold" in APPRECIATION. It's harder to be grateful for every little thing in life than I ever thought it would be.

APPRECIATION THOUGHTS FOR TODAY

1. I'M GRATEFUL I LIVE IN AMERICA, WHERE PEOPLE AREN'T HAVING WARS AND DYING FROM HUNGER.

2. I'M GRATEFUL I'M NOT LIKE BRIDGET'S COUSIN ROBERT.

3. I'M GRATEFUL I'M NOT LIKE AUNT MEG, WHO HAS *EVERYTHING* AND DOESN'T *APPRECIATE ANYTHING*!

Is that negative? It wasn't meant to be. I'm really sorry for Aunt Meg and wish with all my heart I could do something to help her. Imagine the joy of being able buy all the things you wanted, even a new white Porsche. Wow! How sad that she can't appreciate it. I don't know. It's too deep for me. I wonder if I could talk to her about it. Ummm . . . I don't think so.

September 17th—Tuesday—5:20 p.m.

Yesterday was so dull I even forgot to write my three appreciation things. Sorry! I'll write six tonight, okay?

Today Mac and Steven, two of our school's real losers, cornered me and Bridget on our way to the bus. They asked us if we wanted to go to a party tonight. Steven said his friend had a car and *he* wants to go with Bridget.

Bridget and I just turned up our noses and walked away. They said, "Bye, Jennie and BBB." We both knew that meant "big boob Bridget," and it made us both mad but we didn't say anything; it would have just made things worse. Boys are so crude and rude, at least the ones in our school are (they're just down the chain from apes).

Anyway, today was *mostly* a good day. Mom and Dad are getting along better since their trip to Happy Reflection Lake.

OKAY, APPRECIATION TIME.

1. I'M GRATEFUL BRIDGET IS MY VERY NEAREST AND DEAREST FRIEND.

2. I'M GRATEFUL I CAN SEE! WOULDN'T IT BE HORRIBLE TO BE BLIND? I'LL NEVER FORGET ONCE IN GRADE SCHOOL WHEN MISS LAWRENCE BLINDFOLDED EACH OF US AND MADE US TRY TO DO THE THINGS WE ORDINARILY DO. SHE SAID IT WAS ONLY FOR TEN MINUTES BUT IT SEEMED LIKE EONS OF EONS. I HATED IT! I FELT IMPRISONED AND USELESS AND HELPLESS, BUT I THINK EVERYONE SHOULD HAVE THAT EXPERIENCE SO THEY'D KNOW HOW TO *REALLY* APPRECIATE THEIR SIGHT.

3. I'M GRATEFUL THAT MOM AND DAD LIKE EACH OTHER AGAIN. I AM REALLY GRATEFUL FOR THAT!

September 18th—Wednesday—8:30 p.m.

Today was one of the wondrous days of my life. After lunch Bridget and I sat under the old oak tree in front of school and I told her how I'd written in my diary appreciation part that she was my very nearest and dearest friend. We both started crying then because she said she'd written the very same thing in her diary about me. It's like we truly are sisters. Sometimes we pretend to be, and people think we are. We both have long brownish blond hair and sort of greenish eyes but . . . Mother Nature was a little more generous with Bridget in the boob area. Actually, a LOT more generous. I'm as flat in front as I am behind, and I'm short. I hate it!

APPRECIATION THING

1. I APPRECIATE HAVING BRIDGET AS A FRIEND.

2. I APPRECIATE HAVING BRIDGET AS A SISTER (EVEN IF IT IS PRETEND).

3. I APPRECIATE HAVING BRIDGET TO TALK TO. I DON'T KNOW WHAT I EVER, EVER IN THE WORLD WOULD DO WITHOUT HER.

September 21st—Saturday—9:31 a.m.

Sorry I haven't written the last few days but Mrs. Thurber, our English teacher, told us last week she was going to give us a big test on Friday. I've worked hard.

I hope I got an A– or at least a B+ but I don't know. English scares me. I just can't get excited about dangling participles and stuff.

September 22nd—Sunday—2:20 p.m.

Mom and Dad took me out to lunch at the Oakcrest Inn. It was kind of spooky because I could feel they had something deep they wanted to talk to me about, like when they gave me the sex lecture and the drug lecture and the good friends support group lecture, etc., etc., etc.

The Oakcrest Inn is a fancy place. We were all dressed up, and I could feel they were as uncomfortable as I was. I hoped it wouldn't be as awful as their sex lecture. That went on forever, and I still can't figure out exactly how it works. It's sooo gross. Even when we learned about it in school, Bridget and I couldn't figure out the nitty-gritty mechanics of *actually* doing the deed.

Anyway, back to lunch. Mom and Dad stumbled all over each other as they tried to explain that they were having some problems in their marriage. AS IF I DIDN'T KNOW THAT! I was really getting spooked until they told me they were going to start a marriage counseling therapy group. Mom said she really loved Dad but their communication system had broken down or something. One little tear came out of her eye, and Dad reached over and grabbed her hands tightly in his. He told her he felt the same way and they hugged like they would never let go. I felt like an intruder but Dad reached out and pulled me into their hug. That was cozy and warm and family. I was grateful we had a booth. It was like a million, zillion pounds had been lifted off me. I guess I hadn't realized how deeply worried I'd been about them maybe getting a divorce and how hard I'd tried not to let myself think about it. Like if I didn't let myself think about it, it couldn't happen. Dumb, huh?

APPRECIATIONS

---

1. THAT MOM AND DAD ARE GOING TO GET THEIR MARRIAGE STRAIGHTENED OUT.

2. THAT THEY SAID *I WASN'T* RESPONSIBLE FOR THEIR PROBLEMS. (I STILL THINK I AM, THOUGH.)

3. THAT I HAVE A NICE WARM SNUGLY WHITE BED.

September 25th—Wednesday—5:15 p.m.

Marcie Roberts transferred here last week. She's from Washington, D.C., and thinks she's taking over our school and our hockey team and everything else in our (to her) hick town. Everything she does makes me want to throw up . . . but I've got to admit she's a better hockey player than the rest of us put together.

Does that sound like I'm jealous of her? Guess I am. But who wouldn't be? She looks like someone out of *Teen People*, and she's smart, AND HER HOCKEY STICK SEEMS LIKE IT HAS A MAGNET IN IT TO ATTRACT AND CONTROL THE PUCK.

But Bridget has bigger boobs than she has! So there!

Maybe I should try to make friends with Marcie. Maybe part of her would rub off on me. NO! *Bridget's boobs haven't*, and I've been coveting them for about a year. Ugh. Sometimes when I try to be funny I am *so* pathetically *dumb*!

September 26th—Thursday—8:29 p.m.

Same old same old, except Mom and Dad are getting so mushy and giggly that it's revolting. I wonder when they're going to grow up.

October 30th

Mom and Dad tried but my birthday was a bust!

November 2nd—Saturday—9:59 p.m.

I can't believe I haven't written for six weeks—I guess I'm just afraid Mom and Dad *aren't* going to make it—and afraid to let myself believe they will. Crazy, huh?

November 4th—Monday—9:00 p.m.

I don't know who the hamburgerhead is that's trying to put Mom and Dad's marriage back together again but he's Humpty-Dumptying it totally!

Dad's bringing Mom candy when she's on a diet, and she's putting a rosebud in his lapel when she knows damn well he's allergic. I KNOW I SHOULDN'T SWEAR BUT SOMETIMES THAT'S THE ONLY *DAMN* WAY TO VENTILATE. I guess that the whole world, at least our world, is cracking up and flying off in splinters.

I could do a better job than their jerk therapist is doing! I've read some of the kiddy questionnaires he gives Mom and Dad and they scare me, and confuse me, and leave me totally helpless, and HOPELESS AND *EMPTY*!

10:01 P.M.

I had a talk with myself and decided I've *got to have faith* in something, someone. *I've got to start believing* that Dr. Marxley *knows* what he's talking about. He's a professional psychologist, and I'm the dumb kid who has probably caused most of my parents' stress. I don't clean my room, I whine, and pout, and zillions of other things that I'm *not* going to *do again after this very minute*. My changing will probably help Mom and Dad have harmony in their marriage more than anything.

November 5th—Tuesday

I'm trying.

November 6th—Wednesday

Nothing changes.

November 7th—Thursday

Zip.

November 8th—Friday

Nada.

November 9th—Saturday

I've got to get out of this trap.

November 10th—Sunday

Nothing.

November 11th—Monday

More nothing.

November 12th—Tuesday—9:49 p.m.

Haven't written in nine days. Zip to say.

10:22 P.M.

Nada. But I've got my fingers crossed.

November 13th—Wednesday—10:22 p.m.

I'm totally afraid to let myself think the therapy thing is looking pretty good.

November 14th—Thursday

November 15th—Friday

November 16th—Saturday

November 17th—Sunday

November 18th—Monday

November 19th—Tuesday

November 20th—Wednesday—7:10 p.m.

Sorry. Missed another week of writing. It's terror time. I'm still scared to be positive and BEING NEGATIVE HURTS TOO MUCH.

November 21st—Thursday

November 22nd—Friday

November 23rd—Saturday—10:29 p.m.

At last I dare hope, no, ADMIT that Mom and Dad are getting their act together. The therapy sessions *are* working. I'm struggling as hard as I can to keep my end of their marriage up and I'm almost feeling secure again . . . well, a little.

November 24th—Sunday—10:46 p.m.

Haven't written much for forever. Then today— YIKES. I'm in HEAVEN. *BUT* NOW I'M THERE I DON'T KNOW WHAT TO DO. I WANT TO JUMP UP AND DOWN AND SING AND SHOUT AND FLY OR SOMETHING but I guess I should just *quiet down* and think of it as warm belonging and *us* being the loving, comfortable, cuddly family we were always meant to be! OHHHHHHH I am SOOOOOOOOOOOO happy. Happiness is trickling out of my pores and my hair follicles and my fingernails and my toenails. I never, never, ever, ever want this wondrous feeling to end.

I just looked up and even the walls in my house are happy. The doors are smiling and the windows and curtains, even my pajamas are happy. I hadn't noticed in a long time that they have happy HEARTS on them, blue and purple and pink ones for Dad and Mom and Me.

Isn't life scrumptious? We were like a fairy-tale family at Lodge Reflection this weekend, even the sun and the moon and stars obeyed our bidding and *YES*, *YES*, *YES*, "We will live happily ever after!"

November 25th—Monday—6:47 p.m.

I can hardly believe this but today at school while Bridget and I were sitting at the little rickety table in the corner that no one else wants to sit at, we saw Marcie float in like she was Miss America or something. Bridget said, "I'll bet Miss Better-than-anyone-else-in-creation would never eat like *this*," and stuffed half a roll in her mouth, then crammed in some spaghetti, leaving wormy-looking wigglers hanging down her chin. We both cracked up. It was so funny! Funny, that is, until Marcie started walking toward us carrying her tray like it was "laden with precious jewels." Those were Bridget's words, not mine! Anyway, we straightened up as she came toward us, and when she asked if she could sit with us we both nearly lost our cookies.

"Sure," we said as we moved our trays and stuff over to make room for her.

I think Bridget and I both saw the tears floating in front of Marcie's eyes but not spilling over, and we asked in semiunison, "What's the matter? Can we . . . do . . . something . . . ?"

Marcie said softly, "You can! And you are! I just needed to know that everybody's world isn't as black and empty as mine. I mean . . . I know it's not . . . but I feel like it is!" She looked embarrassed, and again Bridget and I both started talking at once, telling her how many times we'd moaned and groaned to each other.

I couldn't believe the look she gave us. "You are soooooooooo lucky," she said. "And so"—she shrugged—"totally together."

We looked at her for a minute to see if she was being sarcastic. When we saw she wasn't, we both started giggling self-consciously. I said, *"We're* probably two of the universe's biggest dorks."

Bridget added, "And for sure two of the world's worst whiners!"

We all three fell apart laughing then and kids at the other tables started looking at us, but we didn't care.

For the rest of the day Marcie hung with us, and we no longer felt she was stuck-up. Actually, we were totally comfortable. It was a nice feeling. She told us how her dad was a high something, I can't remember what, in the army and she'd never lived in one place long enough to feel that she really belonged there. She said every time she saw luggage, even in a store window, she felt shivers race up and down her back.

Marcie couldn't believe it when we told her Bridget and I had been friends since third grade. Bridget even told her how I'd got a sliver in my hand from the swing seat and how she'd taken me weeping to the school nurse my very first day at a new school, in a new town, in a new house.

I frowned. "You don't mention that you just shoved me in with the nurse, who was Dracula's mother, so she could torture and torment me, then you left."

Bridget giggled. "But I did wait outside the door, didn't I!"

Marcie hugged herself like she was cold, and told

us how she'd always had to pretend she was snobbish, like *she didn't need or want friends*, because she was so afraid *no one would want her as one*!

Bridget and I looked at each other for a moment, maybe *really truly appreciating our friendship* for the first time. Then we spit on our right pointer fingers and slapped them on the middle of the palms of our left hands, then we did the same thing in each other's hands, exactly the same way we'd made our special lifelong friendship pact when we were in third grade. When we looked at Marcie she was biting her bottom lip and looking as scared and helpless as I had felt when I first moved here. Almost automatically Bridget and I, at the same time, offered our spitted-on pointer fingers to her. She held out her hands, then returned the gesture, and before we knew it we were all three calling ourselves "Spit sisters" and laughing so hard we were almost falling off our chairs.

7:29 P.M.

Today Bridget and Marcie and I went to the mall after school. Marcie had her mom's credit card. Can you imagine that! She didn't buy much but the clerks all knew her at Dillards and Nordstroms and they treated us like we were somebodies, too! Imagine, ME A SOMEBODY!

November 30th—Saturday—10:14 p.m.

It's Saturday already. Where has the week gone? I love Saturdays, and I think I love this Saturday more than any other Saturday I've lived through. Bridget and I went over to Marcie's for lunch and it was so fancy it was like dining with the Queen of England or somebody. But on the way home Bridget and I decided we like own homes better. Our parents don't have maids and we can sneak in and drink out of the milk carton any time we "feel so inclined," Bridget's words again. We talked about having a maid and decided we'd love it if *she did all the things we didn't want to do* but that probably isn't the way it works. She'd probably be just one more adult to answer to.

BUT . . . back to Marcie's room. She has a mirror on one wall that's twice, maybe almost three times, as big as our full-length mirror in the hall, and she showed us what she learned at the Young Ladies Grooming Academy in France. Bridget said it sounded like dog obedience school, but then we saw the hurt look on Marcie's face. We couldn't get the look to go away until, after we begged for a long time, she started showing us more about how to stand and sit and walk properly. Poor, dumb, stupid, unenlightened us! We didn't even know there was a proper way to stand and sit and walk. But the mirror showed us *there was* and *that* was the reason why Marcie always looked like she was kind of floating when she walked.

Later, Marcie said she's never had so much fun in her life, and Bridget and I trapped the maid with silly questions while Marcie went into the kitchen to sneak some cake and milk. Poor kid, she's not *allowed* to eat between meals. That would cause some friction in our home.

December 4th—Wednesday—7:22 p.m.

What a wonderful Wednesday! It was the maid's day off and Marcie's mom had gone to the country club, la de da! So we spent the afternoon pretending we were entertaining *Ben Affleck* and two of his friends. After a while Marcie got as rowdy and silly as Bridget and me, and we pretended to be doing fancy dancing and all the stuff we'd seen in movies . . . WELL, NOT ALL THE STUFF! Before we left, Marcie hugged us and said she guessed she's never been *taught to be a kid*. Isn't that the strangest thing you've ever heard?

December 5th—Thursday—10:37 p.m.

Marcie came to my house after school and showed Bridget and me a bunch more stuff about walking and talking and eating, but the newness is wearing off. I like Marcie—in fact, I *love* her—but I really feel sorry for her, too. Imagine ME feeling sorry for *her* with her fancy big house, maid, show-off cars, credit cards, and her dad who is writing a *book for the government*. But no one is ever *home* at her house except the maid. My parents had some problems for a while but they are nearly always home for me.

I just called Bridget, even though it's late, and she feels the same way I do.

Marcie is nice and sweet and close and fun but we don't think she can ever be part of our most private world, and we know for sure she could never understand how the *two of us are one*. It's hard for even us to understand.

December 6th—Friday—4:39 p.m.

You won't believe this! Stupid Mac and Paul met me and Bridget at the bus stop and asked us to come to one of their parties. Everyone knows what kind of parties *they* go to. Yuck. We were repulsed. We've laughed all day over it. Every time we pass in the hall or something we say "I'd rather eat dirt," or "I'd rather crawl naked through broken glass," or something else. Paul blew me a kiss when I came out of Mizz Richards's class and I thought I'd throw up right there in the hall. Did I tell you *she* insists we call her *Mizz* instead of Miss. We all wonder if she's a . . . you know.

December 9th—Monday—7:14 p.m.

Bridget and Marcie and I went to the mall, but it's really not that much fun when Marcie can buy *everything* she wants and we can't. We used to have fun *pretending* to buy things but now that just seems stupid and we certainly don't want to share things like that with Marcie. She can feel there's something wrong but we can't tell her what it is. Maybe we're just juvenile and *jealous*. Probably! *Maybe* it's just that we don't want to feel like peasants taking crumbs from Her Majesty when she buys us stuff.

December 10th—Tuesday—11:47 a.m.

I'm home with a miserable head cold. Half the kids at school have it. What a bummer day! I can't believe my house can be so big and cold and scary lonely when there's just me here. It's like there's *nobody here*, not even me!

December 13th—4:47 p.m.

I was home for four of the longest days of my life. I can't believe I would be so *enraptured* to be going back to school. I love that word. I read it in some dumb dull magazine of Mom's I was trying to read when my nose was dripping and my eyes were hardly able to open. But that's OVER AND I'M ME AGAIN! That's good, but Bridget is still sick. I really, really, really miss her. I miss Marcie, too.

December 14th—Saturday—7:42 p.m.

Life is back to normal. The good and the bad of it. The badness of worrying about Mom and Dad and the goodness of looking forward to and preparing for CHRISTMAS. I'm going to talk to Mom tonight about getting our Christmas tree. It used to be such fun when I was little and there was all the mystery and secrets and going to see Santa Claus and really believing in reindeer and the North Pole and elves, and making our special Christmas cookies. It was fun, too, when I got older and started, way in November, looking for presents. Oh I LOVE, LOVE, LOVE CHRISTMAS, at least I used to. I don't know how this one will turn out. Guess I'll just keep my fingers crossed.

December 15th—Sunday—9:59 p.m.

It's been a sad day. Marcie told me and Bridget that her dad has to move back to Washington to finish the last parts of his book. He will be working at the Pentagon and hc's sublet a town house from another officer. Marcie begged her parents to let her stay here with the maid but they wouldn't listen. So what's new? Do parents *ever* listen? Anyway, she said she'd never in her whole life, well, maybe since she was a little tiny kid, felt that she ever belonged anywhere, "had roots," or anything. I can't believe how much she loves Bridget and me after these few months, almost as much as Bridget and I love each other, if that's possible.

I hate to say this but it's almost like Marcie's dying, even though she's just going to be gone for a month or two. But then, like she says, any old time the army wants to move her dad it can, and he always drags her and her mom along if it's not to Africa or someplace like that. He really went there once!

10:51 P.M.

It's almost eleven o'clock and *I'm not* going to let myself think of Marcie leaving us anymore. . . . I'm not . . . I'm not . . . I'm not. . . . *I AM NOT!* It's too sad.

January 1st—Wednesday—9:10 p.m.

Happy New Year? HA!
My whole life is turning upside down and sideways. Marcie has been gone for almost three

weeks, Bridget is spending the holidays at her grandma's, and besides that she's gone mush-brains over Brad Loder. Christmas was a farce because my parents have started giving each other the quiet treatment again.

I'm one lucky puppy! Like the one that got run over by a car instead of a train.

January 7th—Tuesday—8:49 p.m.

I'll admit Brad is sweet to look at but Bridget is acting like a groupie. She's always hanging out in the halls trying to "accidentally" run into him. She's so obvious it's almost a joke!

I hardly saw her all day yesterday and when she did call last night all she could talk about was him! I hate it! I want to be the old *us*! And besides, I think they're moving too fast. I've heard some things about him being a "mover and shaker" (moving in fast on a girl and then shaking her off), and I really don't want her to get hurt. I wonder if all that stuff they taught us in health class really sank in or is she just fluffing it off. Not only that but I know her better than anyone. I *KNOW she doesn't have much self-discipline when she wants something . . .* and she wants him!!

Hey, what am I doing? I'm not her mother! Chill out!!!!

1:21 A.M.

I still can't sleep. Isn't that the dumbest? I've tried eating, watching TV, reading, surfing the Net, and every other stupid thing I can think of but there's some little sticky something itching in my brain about . . . come on, stupid! Check out reality. Are you really all that worried about Bridget or are you just jealous? THAT'S IT! OF COURSE IT IS! I'm just stupid and suspiciously jealous that she LIKES Brad better than she likes me! Isn't that ridiculous? Yes! Okay, so I'm stupid and jealous and ridiculous, what else is new?

January 15th—Wednesday—10:58 p.m.

I haven't written for over a week because I guess I'm too afraid to put my really deep thoughts down on paper. I don't want them to be real! I wish I could *talk* to my mom like I used to when I was little. Then I could tell her, or ask her, anything. Now I'm afraid to talk to her about Dad and embarrassed to talk to her about me and my ditzy problems. Fourteen is a hard age. I'm neither fish nor fowl, kid nor adult. I need someone to DUMP on. I really do! It used to be wonderful when I could just open my mouth and let all my thoughts and emotions and questions out on Mom. She had time for listening then . . . but now . . . well, things have changed. Maybe I should talk to Bridget's mom . . . I don't know. She probably wouldn't have the time or inclination to listen to me, either. Anyway, I know that's dumb. What would I say? That I'm worried? After all, Bridget's *not* a baby . . . besides, she'd hate it if I went behind her back and talked to her mom and she'd probably *hate me forever!*

January 16th—Thursday—8:20 p.m.

After school Bridget asked me to go to the mall with her to pick up some soccer socks, and I was really excited. She hasn't been quite her old self since she met Brad. Well, Bridge and I had just gotten in the south entrance and who was standing there looking in the Gap window . . . Brad, of course! The three of us went to McDonald's. Before we even ordered it seemed like I'd become invisible, and Bridget had that big-eyed silly look on her face as she stared up at Brad like he was a Greek god or something. It made me sick to my stomach, so I slipped away saying I was going next door to the Dollar Store. I'm sure neither one of them even noticed I was gone, or if they did I'm sure they both sighed with relief.

On the way home from the mall Bridget was nervous and quiet. I was uncomfortable and couldn't find anyplace to put my hands. They just hung there like two big useless, in-the-way hams dangling from the ends of my arms, knocking things off the bus seat, and not fitting in my pockets.

Part of me knows I'm just being childish because Bridget has a boyfriend and *I don't* and because she's always "Brad dreaming" instead of being focused on me. I really think *that's* what it is. But in a way I don't know. Some little alarm inside me keeps ringing its head off. I was humiliated when the bus stopped at Bridget's corner and words slipped out of my mouth even though I tried with all my might to keep them in. "Be careful, Bridge," I whispered, feeling stupid and motherish. Then all the way to my stop I berated myself . . . but . . . I still can't stop feeling spooked in some crazy Steven King–book way.

9:10 P.M.

I want to call Bridget and apologize but . . . for what? Sometimes I really am psycho. Guess I'll just try to go to sleep and forget it all. Maybe I'll dream of my own shining knight and then *Bridget and Marcie can both be jealous OF ME!* Oh, I wish I could stop being such a klutz.

Maybe I'll talk to Bridget tomorrow about how I feel, or will that make her stop being my friend? I couldn't stand that. I really never, never, ever could live through that!

January 18th—Saturday—7:01 a.m.

It's Saturday morning, and I know Bridget and her family sleep in on Saturday but I've *got* to talk to her. I hate to wake them all up. Their dog barks his noisy head off when the phone rings. Hmmm . . . I guess I don't *have* to talk to her this second.

8:58 A.M.

I'm going to call in two more minutes, then this dumb feeling I have will be gone and maybe Bridget and I can take a lunch and go on a long bicycle ride. The bike path goes all the way up to Piney Cove. I wonder if we could make it that far.

9:49 A.M.

I'm crushed! Totally and completely *crushed*! Like crumbs in the bottom of the cornflakes box, or worse.

Before I called Bridget I decided I'd make plans for taking Mom's little radio and sandwiches and junk food, and just kind of surprising her . . . but no . . . she had a surprise for me. She told me she and Brad are going on the very same trip I'd planned! Bike path . . . Piney Cove . . . everything . . . just like she'd read my mind and swiped my idea. I HATE HIM! HATE HIM! HATE HIM AND *HER* TOO! Of course, I don't really. I'm just sad and mad at myself. It's probably *me* I hate.

January 19th—Sunday—6:02 p.m.

I picked up yesterday's mail and in it was a long really personal letter from Marcie. She's met a guy in her class who likes her. *What's not to like?* I miss her like anything. *What's wrong with me* that no guys like me?

January 21st—Tuesday—8:06 p.m.

Bridget is beginning to sympathetically dole out a little more time to me. I feel like a street person, a beggar kneeling gratefully to thank her for her crumbs.

January 24th—Friday—10:10 p.m.

I've started hanging some with Silver. Her name is really Sarah Silverman, but she says everyone's been calling her Silver since she can't even remember when.

She's on our hockey team and she's a good player, but she's different from anyone else I've ever been close to. I know this sounds snobby but . . . she's not very clean, and her clothes are kind of wrong, and she didn't seem to want to tell me where she lives. Her grammar isn't very good, but beggars can't be choosers and I'd rather have *any kind of a friend* than no *friend at all*. Besides, she's funny, and I need whatever I can get *of that* in my life right now. In a way this friendship is a little strange but maybe that's because I need *something* strange in my life. *Right now I'm feeling kind of like a lonely, left out nothing floating nowhere but down down down.*

10:41 P.M.

I've had enough of this negative, feel-sorry-for-myself crap! Tomorrow I'm going to start being the other ME! I wish I had someone to talk to about how I can be *another me*, and I wish I wasn't so skinny and short. I look like a baby.

January 27th—Monday—9:36 p.m.

I'm not sure I can handle *this*. I'm really not! Not on top of everything else. It can't be true. It simply CAN NOT!!!!!!!!!! It's like the rottenest of all nightmares. Me coming in from school trying to put a smile on my face and some sunshine in my heart and what did I see? Mom slumped in the corner, by the stove, like a bag of wet wash. At first I thought she'd had a heart attack or something. My heart was beating wildly and I wondered who I should call first: Dad or 911. The sounds coming out of Mom's mouth didn't make any sense at all. Fear began to strangle me in a giant snake grip. I could almost *see* it! Finally words began to dribble out. "Mom . . . Mom, talk to me . . . Shall I call the doctor . . . an ambulance . . . do you want . . . some . . . water?"

It seemed like all of the eternities mixed into one before Mom slobbered, her eyes and nose and mouth flushing like a toilet. "Your dad . . . he's . . . he's . . ."

"He's what? Tell me what, Mom."

She didn't answer. I could see my dad in his casket, his face white as snow, with a bullet in his head from a drive-by shooter. I'm so dumb.

Finally I crumpled down beside Mom and whispered, "*Please* . . . Mom, tell me?"

"He's . . . he's . . . left . . . us," she whispered back.

Mom looked like a frightened, frozen, lost little child, and I scrunched down and took her in my arms, wiping away her tears and telling her that everything would be all right, that together we could work it out. I could feel myself becoming the mother figure and wondered how that could possibly be.

It's too horrible to be real. Just too, too horrible and scary and lonely. How will Mom and I ever, ever get along without Dad? Why did he leave? Doesn't he love Mom anymore? Doesn't he love me? Does he have a . . . girlfriend? Does she have a daughter he loves more than me? One who is all the good things I'm not! *How can thoughts hurt so much when they aren't even physical!*

I'm sick. I'M REALLY SICK! Will I ever heal?

11:48 P.M.

I'm so tired. Every particle of my body aches but I can't go to sleep because my mind just keeps darting and dashing and splashing and racing. Why? Why? Why? I *know why* but I'm too tired to try to make sense out of something so nonsensical.

January 28th—Tuesday—4:46 p.m.

I can't believe Mom and I got up, did our thing, ate breakfast, and took off for school and work *without ever mentioning yesterday and last night.* We barely said anything, and I was too scared to ask any questions. I wonder if I look as pale and aged to her as she does to me? Does she hurt and feel as empty as I do? Could she possibly?

January 29th—Wednesday—8:32 p.m.

My life has taken on a completely gray color and almost a mechanical existence of its own. Inside I feel cold and dead but outside I'm doing all the things that are required of me. It's scary . . . *like somebody I don't know has become me!* I wish Mom and I could talk it out, but we can't at all. Not one word. She's *STOIC*; I had that word once in spelling, and it's exactly how she is—showing no emotion or grief, joy or pain. At least *I sometimes* forget for a minute or two.

January 30th—Thursday—4:55 p.m.

Mom is taking pills that the doctor prescribed. I hate them because they make her seem like she's not really Mom. We still haven't mentioned Dad. It's like he doesn't exist anymore except in my bleeding heart. I wonder why he doesn't phone or write or something. I wonder why he hates me. What did I do? What did I say? I want to ask him. To plead with him to forgive me for whatever it is. I love him sooooo much and miss him more than he can ever imagine!

January 31st—Friday—6:22 a.m.

I'm beginning to *hate* Dad. How can he be so selfish and mean and cruel to Mom and me? We aren't ALL THAT BAD! I'm so confused. I wish I could figure out if I hate him more than I love him or . . . love him more than I hate him! Or . . . if I even care one *damn* stinking bit one way or the other.

February 1st—Saturday—3:32 p.m.

How can everything be so dark when the sun is shining? The sky is dark, the buildings are dark, people are dark. It is a depressing, no-meaning existence and I feel . . . totally helpless and alone in it. Is the rest of my life going to be this empty, leaky bucket kind of existence?

Why doesn't Dad phone? Why doesn't he write or E-mail? Is he going to divorce us? These crazy thoughts are crashing and smashing through my head all the time. Bashing everything else out.

February 3rd—Monday—4:58 p.m.

Lots of the kids I know at school are divorced but they don't seem as devastated as I'll be if it happens to us. Or are they really feeling as crushed and run-over and brain-dead as I am *but* they're just putting on a lying front, and inside they really do feel the same? I can't believe that. It doesn't show! But then maybe they are just like me, *bleeding* on the inside, where people can't see it.

February 5th—Wednesday—9:32 p.m.

Bridget's boyfriend, Brad, got an afternoon and Saturday job at the sports store his uncle owns. So now she has some time for me. I'm sooooo appreciative of her wonderful and caring friendship! She knows something is wrong but I can't talk about that for now. Wish I could!

February 6th—Thursday—7:41 p.m.

Today I finally unloaded about Dad to Bridge. She truly is *my bridge over troubled water*. We sang that song one year in choir and I thought it was sweet and deep then, but now it is even deeper and sweeter. Bridge and I hugged and cried together, and while it was sad it was really wonderful and healing too, kind of like the tears were washing away part of my pain. I am so fortunate to have someone like her for a friend. I wish I could do the same with Mom but I can't! She's locked herself away somewhere inside herself. Dad must hate us both a lot to just disappear. I wish . . . But wishes don't come true. I found that out when I was seven years old and my cat ran away.

February 7th—Friday—9:01 p.m.

Bridget had thought Brad was going to work late doing inventory but that's tomorrow night, so of course she dumped me and our plans to go to the mall for pizza and a movie. That shows where I stand in her life! She apologized and said she knew I'd understand . . . but I don't! I *don't want to*! I need her *now*! After I've spilled my guts out to her you'd think she'd understand, but no one does. Not one single person in the whole universe cares one single bit about stupid, nothing, nobody me.

10:10 P.M.

I wonder how long a person needs to cry to get dehydrated to death? Is that possible? If it is I'm on my way and I don't care! At least Mom's zombied out on the pills her doctor gives her and can't *feel anything*! Maybe I'll go sneak some just to see what happens to me. NO, I think I'd rather hurt than feel nothing. *Not feeling* seems as scary as *not being*. I'm making less sense than I usually do.

Talking to myself is like talking to the brain-dead.

I guess that's what I am. And yet I am the best I've got. Yuck. Ugh.

February 10th—Monday—4:47 p.m.

I don't know when I've ever felt this good and nourished and appreciated in my whole life! I went to school practically crawling on my belly, I felt so low, and then I got into Miss Marress's class and met the most vibrant, witty, happy-go-lucky substitute teacher who has ever been placed on earth. Since I was in the front row he asked me to pass out some papers for a pop math quiz, and everyone groaned like we were being tortured. Groaned, that is, till they started looking at the papers. When they calmed down the new teacher introduced himself as Jonathan Johnstone.

The test had a few simple math problems with some questions about ourselves in between. Some of the questions were funny, some were serious, and some were hurty kid questions that I'm sure all of us have asked ourselves.

It was obvious from the first minute that Mr. Johnstone knew worlds more about kids than most teachers.

When it was time to turn in the quiz Mr. Johnstone told us that he hoped we all scored ourselves high on question number 14 because that was the *one* question the *whole quiz* would be graded upon.

All of us looked surprised as we checked our papers. Number 14 said, "In life what number are you on a scale from 1 to 14?"

The room was quiet for a second.

Then Mr. Johnstone started laughing like he'd heard the funniest joke in the world and said, "Next time I have *that* question on a test—and I *will*—I WANT EACH OF YOU TO BE *FOURTEENS*, OR AT LEAST MORE THAN TENS! *EVEN IF YOU'RE HAVING A TOTALLY ROTTEN DAY!*"

Everybody laughed comfortably and he passed out little candy bars. Then he asked us subtraction and addition and multiplication problems regarding a truckload of candy bars, and we were all better than we thought we were or, maybe just better because Mr. Johnstone was *bringing out the best in us*!

This is a secret that I could only tell Bridget or Marcie but since they're both unavailable at the moment, I'll tell you, diary.

I'm sorry Miss Marress's mother in Florida had a stroke and is sick, but in a way I'm *HAPPY that she is sick*, too, so we get to have Mr. Johnstone for math.

I know *that's* sick but that's how it is.

February 11th—glorious Tuesday—4:57 p.m.

I couldn't wait to get to school. I was wondering what funny jokes Mr. Johnstone would tell us. It's unusual to have such an energetic, funny, happy, understanding person *for a teacher*! Usually they're kind of dull and dowdy, but I guess I shouldn't expect them to all be handsome professional-type *entertainers and educators* like Mr. Johnstone is.

I dashed into math class before anyone else, and Mr. Johnstone seemed as glad to see me as I was to see him. I'm really glad I'm good in math.

February 19th—Wednesday—5:01 p.m.

Bridget has been grounded because she sneaked out with Brad, but tomorrow she will be out of house imprisonment and I'll be *gladder than glad*! It's no fun going to the mall alone. There's no one to . . . I don't know . . . it's just nice to have a real comfortable old friend to . . . you know. I wish she was in Mr. Johnstone's class, too. Bridget's mom has been driving her to school and picking her up. Often she even picks her up for lunch. It's disgusting, but like Bridget says, her folks are VERY strict. I'd hate that! My folks . . . I'm *not* thinking about that anymore.

On to the good part of my life! Mr. Johnstone kept rubbing his right eye during class and at one point asked me if I'd stay for a minute after the bell rang. I wondered what in the world he'd ever want to talk to me about and spent the rest of the class wondering what I'd done, hoping I hadn't offended him or done something childishly stupid like I so often do. When the last kid had left he touched my hand lightly and told me how impressed he was by my *"superior ability and positive attitude."* Then he asked me if I would like to be HIS AIDE! Can you believe that? Help him correct papers and stuff till his eye heals. He got something in it that scratched the cornea so he's going to have to wear dark glasses till it's better. Isn't that the greatest? Well, maybe not for him but certainly THE greatest for me. And he's already okayed it with Principal Doney.

February 20th—Thursday—9:20 p.m.

Bridge has been freed from her incarceration and we were like two little puppies off our leashes as we dashed from one store to another in the mall. She even insisted on buying me a notepad, and we tried on everything that looked wearable. It was totally fun, and we laughed about the things we liked and didn't like. I am soooooo glad to have her back.

Oh, Mr. Johnstone had to go to a faculty meeting after school so I couldn't start aiding him today. *I hope tomorrow!!!!!* Besides, he wanted me to get an okay from my mom. No sweat there.

February 21st—Friday—4:36 p.m.

I got to help Mr. Johnstone correct papers today after school, and it was awesome. I can't believe how totally cool he is and how kind and ego-boosting. With every sentence he spoke he seemed to say something that made me feel like a better person! A nicer person! A smarter person! AN IMPORTANT *ME*!

9:32 P.M.

Bridge and I just got home from a thoroughly dumb movie. We were bugged all through it by Mac and Steve throwing popcorn in our hair and trying to get our attention in every other childish silly way. They are soooo immature. I wish there were more males like Mr. Johnstone. Maybe there will be in a couple of thousand years if mankind lives that long.

February 23rd—Sunday—8:23 p.m.

What a boring miserable day. We had to go see Mom's sister, my Aunt Meg. It was kind of weird how it seemed like Mom *could only* talk about how worried she was about Aunt Meg, and I absolutely *could not* force myself to talk about how worried I was about *her*. We were both really uncomfortable coming and going. It's a funny feeling because we used to be really close.

Isn't it strange how time passes so slowly when you're bored. I wish it was Monday and time to go to school. Actually, to *Mr. Johnstone's class*! Mom's become someone I don't know. I'm lonely.

February 24th—Monday—7:14 p.m.

Today after school I was helping Mr. Johnstone correct papers and work up another quiz when a brilliant little sunbeam sparkled its way into a bluish green vase on his desk. He stopped what he was doing, and touching my shoulder, whispered, "Shhhhh, Jennie," as he pointed to the sunbeam. It was magnificent. It almost seemed like multicolored lights were coming from *inside* the vase. "It's beautiful," I whispered back. He touched my hair so softly I could more sense the touch than really feel it. "It's not half as beautiful as you are, precious little Jennie. Never in all your life allow yourself to forget that."

My heart is singing the Hallelujah Chorus with a thousand backup singers. There would be no problem children in all the world if they each had a Mr. Johnstone for a teacher—or preacher or leader or whatever.

His concepts are so wondrous I can hardly contain them.

February 25th—Tuesday—9:19 p.m.

I've had a busy day. I helped Mr. Johnstone for an hour after school, and he really lights up my life, like the little sunbeam. I will *never forget THAT* experience! It's almost too sacred to talk about.

Back to reality. After helping Mr. J, I met Bridge at the craft shop and we bought some pretty little flower stickers to put on special invitations her mom is going to send out for a party she's having. I was really impressed her mom trusted her that much and I told her so. See, some of Mr. J's self-worth teachings are rubbing off on me already. I wish I could tell Mom exactly how I feel about him . . . but she wouldn't understand. It would just sound dumb. Maybe if she was home like Bridget's mom. No! *She's* not perfect, either. I know! Bridget tells me. Wanna hear a secret? I guess only Mr. Johnstone is perfect!!!

February 26th—Black Wednesday—7:21 p.m

I walked into Mr. Johnstone's room with a smile on my face and a warmth inside me all over—that is, until I saw Miss Marress sitting at *his* desk. I don't know when I've ever been so angry and frustrated. Talk about childish! After all, *it is* dull, dreary, dowdy Miss Marress's room! Mr. Johnstone was just a substitute. JUST A SUBSTITUTE, but he was probably the only person in the world who could have brought out all the good in me until I TRULY COULD have become anything I ever dreamed of becoming. I guess kids are meant to get the short end of the stick most of their lives, whatever that means.

March 1st—Saturday—11:49 p.m.

I've been just dragging around for a couple of days, and if I didn't feel so sorry for Miss Marress I'd feel more sorry for myself. She's kind of like the pumpkin in Cinderella that the magnificent magic carriage turned back into. Does that make sense? I guess it doesn't matter since I'm the only one interested or un-interested. Whatever.

12:01 P.M.

I was just finishing lunch when the phone rang. Guess who? Marcie! SHE'S HOME! TO STAY RIGHT HERE WITH ME AND BRIDGE FOR THE REST OF HER LIFE! I'm so happy I don't know whether to laugh or cry. I think I'll laugh! After Mr. Johnstone left I didn't think I'd *ever* laugh again.

Marcie's coming over right after she finishes her lunch and gets some things unpacked. I'll be soooo glad to have her here!!! I need her. Bridget has put me so far down on her list I barely belong there at all. I wonder how I'll tell Marcie about Mom and Dad.

1:21 P.M.

What's happened to Marcie? Why doesn't she hurry?

March 2nd—Sunday—3:30 p.m.

When Marcie finally got to my house we about hugged each other silly. Then we danced and giggled and laughed so loudly Mom came in to see what was happening. She seemed like the old Mom again, and after a lot of begging called Marcie's mom to ask if Marcie could sleep over. Sleep? We talked almost the whole night. Her dad is in Germany for a few weeks and then will be in Italy, and my dad is like, who knows where, doing who knows what. He doesn't write or phone or E-mail or anything. It's very sad and it hurts a lot. Marcie's hurting, too, because her boyfriend, Kyle, had to go with his parents to Hawaii where his dad had been sent. He's in the service, too. Then we talked about good wonderful things like her staying here forever and Bridget and Mr. Johnstone. I think about him a lot.

March 4th—Tuesday—11:12 p.m.

Mom took Bridget and Marcie and me to a concert, but it wasn't one of the big ones we really wanted to go to.

March 5th—Wednesday—12:01 p.m.

I just woke up thinking I had heard Mom and Dad quarreling. They were both trying to shush each other but it was obvious the old tensions were back. Half asleep, I tried to, with mental telepathy, encourage them to again go back to the marriage counselor and straighten everything out. . . . Then I woke up completely and now I'm lying here having to face reality! He's gone!

At one point long, long ago, Mom and Dad were working really hard to get things together and *I* was absolutely no help to them, in fact, I'm sure I caused more troubles and friction than anything else in the world ever could. I don't know why I can't be kinder and nicer and cleaner and more respectful and not so talk-backish and all the other horrible negative things I've always been. No wonder he never writes or calls or anything.

Why can't I be more like Mr. Johnstone? Ummmmm, maybe I can try. I wish he'd been here longer. Mr. Johnstone was such a wonderful, *wonderful* example for me! I will *never* forget him! If he had been here longer to teach me I could probably have helped Mom and Dad to know how good and honorable and wonderful they both are. I'm so cranky and unappreciative and such a handicap to them! I wonder if I hadn't been born would things have been better for them. Probably! Tears, tears, please wash away my fears.

March 6th—Thursday—7:52 p.m.

Marcie had to go somewhere with her mom, so after school Bridget and I walked out to the little grove behind the Methodist church. It's a beautiful quiet place and we both needed to talk. We'd told our moms we were going to the mall, but today *that* seemed totally unimportant because we were both feeling sad and serious. Bridge was desolated because Brad just up and dumped her for Amy Tines. I've got my mom-and-dad problems as well as the Mr. Johnstone emptiness in my life. I guess *he's* the only *truly trustworthy* adult I've ever known. We wondered if parents ever took time to consider how much kids hurt. Like Bridget said she totally *couldn't* talk about Brad to her mom. Still she said all the stuff connected with him "hung like big rocks in her mind and belly" and she didn't know how to get them out.

That opened the door for me to confide in her deeply and completely how much I worshiped Mr. Johnstone; how he'd become the power in my life that held me together both physically and mentally, and how I'd probably completely dissolve into a puddle of nothing without his strength and caring.

Hidden in the grove, Bridge and I clung to each other like lost kids in a witchy scary fairy tale and bawled our eyes out! Her about Brad and me about my dad's leaving and maybe divorcing us and . . . Mr. Johnstone. I felt like I was being cut up in little pieces. Would part of me go to Dad and part to Mom, or would neither one of them want me and I'd have to go to a foster home? I'd read in the paper about a couple who got fed up with their kid and just drove off and left him at a service station. Maybe I'll have to go to my drunken Aunt Mcg—that would teach me!

Bridget comforted me as I needed to be comforted, and the pain sort of wheezed out of me like air from a balloon. We didn't have answers for any of our problems, but at least it was good to have someone to talk to. That helped a whole lot.

In a way I feel guilty as sin about not being able to help Bridge more. She *wants to hate* Brad but she can't. She still loves him, and if I told her what a stupid jerk I've always thought he was that would hurt her even worse. Why can't more people be like Mr. J? He'd never hurt anybody. He'd just help them solve their problems and live happily from then on.

After a while Bridget suddenly curled up on the grass in a tight little hard ball and sobbed like . . . well, like nothing I've ever heard before or ever care to hear again. Her torment was so great it was tangible. I literally could feel big, hard, cold, rugged chunks of it. And there was nothing I could do except curl up around her and coo gentle loving sounds like my mom had done to me in the far far away and long long ago.

1:01 A.M.

I am *not* going to think of *my* problems and Bridget's one single more time. I am wiping them out of my head absolutely and completely, detaching myself from the whole sordid mess before they drive me stark raving mad. I'm going to totally quit taking on my parents' problems, too! THEY ARE *THEIR PROBLEMS,* NOT MINE!

I think I'll take one little black box compartment of my mind and toss into it anything in my life I can't handle! YEP! That's the only safe and sound way to keep my *mental boat* afloat. Right?

7:01 A.M.

Gotta go. Mom in her monotone haze is calling me for breakfast and telling me I'll be late for my bus. I WILL NOT EVER THINK OF ANY OF THE AWFUL

THINGS IN MY LIFE AGAIN!!! EVER!!! I'LL JUST
LET THEM LAY THERE AND ROT!!! SO THERE!!!

March 7th—Friday—5:27 p.m.

Bridget and I are doing pretty well. I told her
about the little black box in my head where I store all
the crap in my life, and she's started doing the same.
Now those things aren't even part of us, they are just
the trash that *needs* to be locked away from everything
sunshiny and good.

This afternoon after John Bonham had said some
crude things to me in the hall I decided to take those
hateful feelings out on the hockey puck. I named the
puck "Flusher" and pretended it was anything or
anyone I hate. Then I slammed the heck out of it.
Marcie and Bridget were impressed with my new
power and they asked me what was going on. Then
they decided to do it too. It's really a cool way to get
rid of aggressions. We did some spot shooting, naming
the puck after Brad, my father . . . or anyone who at
the moment was bugging us.

Afterward the three of us went down to Blake's
Bakery and stuffed ourselves. We made a solemn pact
that when we go to college we'll room together even
if that means we *can't* be in a sorority. Marcie says
most sororities only have space for two people in a
room. We joked about how we were going to decorate
and that we'd probably only have one car, which we'd
take turns driving.

It was sweet till Marcie said *she'd probably never*
be able to be with us because by then her parents would
most likely be stationed in China or Germany or who

knows where. We would have comforted her but the bus drew up to her stop just then. It was sad. But I think her parents will let her go with us. I know she'll feel that way, too, when she takes a little time to think about it.

9:19 P.M.

I've been lying here looking at the moon and stars out my window. They are so beautiful and shiny that I know God is in his Heaven and all is right with the world, as the poem says. This is a good and wonderful feeling, and I never want it to end. I want it to stand still! Right here! For forever! Like my hero Mr. Johnstone said, *"Life is good if we savor the pleasant, flavorful moments."* I MISS HIM SOOOOOO MUCH!!!!!! I wish he was here right now to share this particularly lovely feeling. It's almost like the little sunbeam on the vase.

March 10th—Monday—4:48 p.m.

You will not believe what happened today!!! I straggled into math class early because some of the guys were messing around in the hall and guess WHO was there? I didn't even notice him standing by the door until I felt his almost electric hand on my shoulder.

"Why so forlorn, precious, beautiful little princess?" he asked softly, almost as though he felt what I felt. Then he offered to help me if I ever needed his help. It was one of the most wondrous moments in my life. Did I need his help? Did I want his help? Do I need oxygen? Just as I started to open my mouth Mr. Johnstone backed away because kids were running down the hall toward us. I wanted to slam the door shut in their faces and have Mr. Johnstone all to myself. But of course, I'm not that dumb, so I floated to my desk. Imagine having Mr. Johnstone for our sub a second time! We're the luckiest kids in the whole wide world! Miss Marress's mother is sick again. I hope she—no I don't mean that!

8:17 P.M.

Just before the class closing bell rang Mr. Johnstone told us he'd have to leave before us to go to a staff meeting. I felt really bad because all during class I'd been sitting two inches off my chair waiting for the time I'd be alone with him. But it was okay, too, because I also couldn't wait to get home and look up *forlorn* in the dictionary. I wasn't sure what it meant. Well, now I've looked it up, and I absolutely cannot believe that he would know exactly how I felt.

1. LEFT BEHIND, ABANDONED, DESERTED.

2. IN PITIFUL CONDITION, WRETCHED, MISERABLE.

3. WITHOUT HOPE, DESPERATE.

4. BEREFT OR DEPRIVED.

Isn't he amazing? It's almost scary. He's so . . . so . . . the only word I can think of that almost fits him is *spiritual*. Sort of like Mother Teresa. Someone who really loves and understands people and wants to help them. I'm sure *most* adults don't have any idea how painful growing up is for us kids, but *he* understands completely.

I remember vividly when Mr. Johnstone was here before as a sub, and Gordo, who had just moved here from Mexico, couldn't read the section when it was his turn to read. Mr. Johnstone didn't shrug him off or embarrass him or anything. He just walked to Gordo's desk, put his arm around his neck, and told him what a great guy he was and how proud of him he was that he was working so hard to fit into his place in America. Then he looked at the whole class seriously and said gently, "And *we each* feel privileged to help you, don't we, class?" We each made our own affirmative noise, even Billy Gregson and Del de Hyatt, two of the world's biggest and baddest bullies.

March 11th—Tuesday—9:59 p.m.

I wonder what makes Mr. Johnstone so different. Maybe it's because we can trust him. I trust him emphatically! I honestly think he's the most perfect person I've ever met!

March 12th—Wednesday—7:16 p.m.

Mr. Johnstone has permission from the principal to use me as his aide again. I feel so honored and privileged. *He is the one* the writer wrote about in the old song "You Light Up My Life." I'm sure there can't be another person as everything wonderful as he is . . . or is there? Hopefully there are many, many, many Mr. Johnstones around to help kids . . . but I doubt it . . . I've never seen any. And he *needs* me with his bad eye and all, isn't that incredible?

When I was little, I used to think my dad was perfect, but now I know he's just another *ME FOR ME* and I hate his guts. I don't really, though. Mr. Johnstone wouldn't approve of that, and besides, somewhere deep inside me, all the goodness of Dad is still with me. Maybe someday he'll come back to us. I wish I knew how to really, really pray. Maybe someday I can talk to Mr. Johnstone about that and my family and . . . even Mom and her pills. Talking to Mr. Johnstone—the summation of all things good!

March 13th—Thursday—10:17 p.m.

Today Mr. Johnstone said the principal had rethought allowing me to be his aide and decided it wasn't prudent.

I just looked up *prudent* in the dictionary: "1. capable of exercising sound judgment in practical matters. 2. cautious or discreet in conduct; circumspect; sensible; not rash. *syn* see CAREFUL, WISE."

None of that stuff makes any sense. Mr. Johnstone is the most practical, discreet, circumspect, sensible person I know. I guess they've just got these stupid school rules that are only made up to hurt kids.

I feel so kicked out of the celestial circle! I have no idea what that means but I read it once.

I wish it weren't so late so I could call Bridget or

Marcie . . . but *it is* too late. Their parents would kill me if I called after ten—unless someone had died!

I was so desperate for someone to talk to that I tiptoed into Mom's room, but she was laid out like a log, snoring with crud drooling out the side of her mouth and down her chin. It's so disgusting. She looks like an unjointed puppet, sprawled out grotesquely half on and half off the bed. There's an open pill bottle on her nightstand.

There has to be something I can do to help her. Something that will help her help herself *so she can help me*! I think I'll call Uncle Harry. Maybe he can help his druggy sister-in-law more than he can help his alcoholic wife. Honestly, though, I don't think anyone can help! Not one of them!

I'm ashamed I wrote that *and I should be*! Mom's not anything as bad as I make her seem. Actually, I think she functions all right during the day and it's just at night when she's home that she escapes from all her troubles, *including me*, with those damn, damn, damn, damn pills. I HOPE THAT'S IT! I REALLY THINK IT IS! *IT MUST BE!* Oh, dear God, please let it be because I don't know what I'd do if she lost her job.

Oh tears, tears, tears please stop.

You've turned to ice

And you are cutting up my heart.

When will you end?

Why did you start?

What lies before me on my way?

And—

Can I make it through another day?

I remember once our English teacher told us a poem had to be written from the very deepest emotion to be good. I'll never write another one! It hurts too much, and heaven knows we don't need any more pain on this planet: Marcie being dragged around the world kicking and screaming; and Bridge, dear, dear Bridge, who wouldn't hurt a flea, being dumped like she was rotting garbage; and me . . . first Dad, then Mom, then my sacred, wonderful friend, Mr. Johnstone. If only I were allowed to work with him I'm sure he could help me straighten everything out. Maybe I could even have him talk to Mom. He's so levelheaded and makes such sense I'm sure he could help her get her life cleaned up.

Why won't the principal let me be Mr. Johnstone's aide? That is soooooo asininely stupid! Maybe he's jealous of Mr. Johnstone's wonderful gift and how we students are drawn to him and dearly love and respect him and we'd do anything for him. Even the demon, Del de Hyatt, acts almost human in his class. I'm totally amazed that adults can sometimes have such poor judgment.

March 14th—BLACK FRIDAY!

Miss Marress is back and Mr. Johnstone is *gone*! I feel totally useless! Worthless! I wanted so much to *work with him*, to *be with* him, TO *BE LIKE HIM*! I wish Marcie and Bridget could have been in his class. HE would have *empowered* all of us. Instead, feeling like three rejects, we collapsed on the grass by the little stream that runs by the school fence and ate our lunch. We *really did not* hear the bell! I guess we were so mesmerized by feeling sorry for ourselves we weren't aware of anything else in the whole world. Maybe it was good therapy for us, though. Because after we'd gone over and over and over the rottenness and unfairness of all the messy things we were living through, we finally started to snicker a little. We were late going back to our classes and were caught by a grounds monitor and given citations. We just laughed. Citations seemed minor relative to our *real* problems!

When we got to the east school door we noticed that someone had parked outside the fence and was playing loud country music on a car stereo. Bridget giggled and started line dancing, making up her own words as she sang to the music: "Brad dumped me, your dad dumped you, but we'll stand together 'cause we're true blue."

Marcie joined her: "My cat got lost, my dog got stole, but we're helpin' each other get out of our hole."

Suddenly, realizing we could be in terrible trouble, we ran back to our classes. Halfway there Marcie stopped suddenly and said in a country drawl, "I reckon if we could get some weed somewhere we could probably blow off the whole load of our gol-darn troubles to hell and back."

At first I didn't want to use drugs. I told Marcie and Bridget how once I'd become a sort-of friend to Silver and she had taken me to a party. It was in a grungy little basement apartment down by Mr. Miller's warehouse. When we first opened the door the smell was awful, and it was so dark and loud and scary that I sneaked out as soon as I could and ran all the way back to Orchard Avenue to catch a bus home.

I couldn't even go near Silver after that. I know it wasn't her fault but . . . I dunno . . . it was kind of a nightmarelike experience that I've been trying to pretend never happened.

Anyway, Marcie said she'd smoked MJ a few times when they were stationed in Germany, but then her dad found out about it and she was whipped off to a private school, as if they wouldn't have drugs there!

9:21 P.M.

Marcie and Bridge and I met at Snider's Ice Cream Palace and sat at the little table way in the corner that's practically a private room of its own. Our moms thought we were at the movies. We could talk at the Palace without having every word heard. We decided smoking a little MJ couldn't hurt us and would make our troubles float away. We got so excited we almost couldn't wait, but we knew we had to put together a really careful game plan.

I hesitatingly offered to talk to Silver. That was going to be kind of weird because we didn't want her to be one of us, but even more, we don't want to go to any of the pushers at school.

March 17th—Monday—6:37 p.m.

It was easier than I thought. I just pretended to accidentally bump into Silver after our gym class. We pulled away a little from everybody and I tried to sound casual as I asked her where I could get a little grass. She asked me what kind I wanted and told me more than I wanted to know about it. Finally she said she'd meet me tomorrow afternoon at the Gap in the mall with some Mellow Yellow.

7:39 P.M.

I wasn't that scared at first but now I'm getting scareder by the minute. All the what-ifs are piling in on me like avalanches. What if the cops . . . ? What if some tattletale at school . . . ? What if the principal . . . ? What if Mom . . . ? What if one of Marcie's or Bridget's parents . . . ? They'd never let me be friends with them again. That would kill me. It literally would! Maybe we shouldn't do it. But everybody does! And why is it any worse for me to use a little marijuana than it is for Mom to use her escape pills? What's the difference?

March 18th—Tuesday—8:01 a.m.

I just decided I'm *not* going to meet Silver!

8:28 A.M.

I just decided I *am* going to meet Silver! I promised Marcie, Bridget, and Silver, and I can do it! But I don't know when I've ever *felt like this*! I'm shaking.

6:31 P.M.

This has been the longest day in creation, but finally school was over and I was at the mall. I tried to look casual as I sauntered into the Banana Republic and then the Gap. I had to be normal and cool on the outside but inside I felt volcanic. Especially after I walked into the Gap and Silver yelled out so loudly everyone could hear: "Hey, Jennie, you left your notebook on the bus bench."

I felt as if everyone in the mall had their suspicious eyes on us, but I guess no one did. I thanked her and slipped the money she'd asked for into her hand, then said good-bye and took the notebook and the little Target sack. I wanted to run as fast as I could for the bus stop, but some inner force controlled me, and I slowly put the notebook and sack in my backpack and pretended to look at a shirt. It's weird how I seem to have a little nanny or something inside me that takes over when my mind turns to mush.

7:20 P.M.

I just called Marcie and Bridget and asked them if they wanted to go bicycling Saturday. That meant I had completed my mission, the signal that I had the stuff! *I feel* like I've just had a small part in the *Mission: Impossible* movie.

March 19th—Wednesday—1:01 p.m.

Short day at school—teachers' meeting. Wow for us! Mom is scurrying around trying to get herself off to a convention which will last till late tonight. I'm fluttering about like a caged little sparrow trying to be helpful but mostly just getting in the way.

Things couldn't have worked out better. We're so organized there's no way anyone *but us* will know what we're doing. Wow! We're gong to smoke on the back porch in our underwear, with shower caps on our hair so we won't reek of smoke, and we're *not* going to overdo the thing. Marcie and Bridget are coming over right after they get their chores done. And *our moms* think we're gonna study. HA!

10:07 P.M.

Mom should be coming in any time now but it's okay. Everything is under control. In fact, it's soooooo controlled. I'd like to stay this way for the rest of my life.

I didn't understand that marijuana was such an enlightening drug. I comprehend completely now why Mom wants to, actually *HAS TO*, use her prescription drugs. It's what kept her on track after Dad left. But I'm not mad at him, either. He's just out there blowing in the wind and doing what he has to do. Everything is sooooo cool and you get everything in its right perspective. Cool Mom, I'll be so glad to see her, but scared, because I'm still kind of upped. I wonder if she'll recognize it. I guess I better be careful. This thing is too good to blow. *So good,* in fact, I smoked another short one after B & M left.

March 27th—Thursday—11:42 p.m.

I can't believe it's been a week since Bridge and Marcie and I started our little excursions into Happy Land. It's funner even than Disneyland in its own cool no-hassle way.

At school we three have our little secret signs to each other in the hall, even in the classes we have together. It's a mysterious world that no one else has a key to. I love it! Love it! Love it! And life isn't nearly as bumpy as it used to be.

March 28th—Friday—6:33 p.m.

I didn't get my assignment in by Wednesday, when it was due, so I was treated like Dumbo in the movie. *Like* school is the most important thing in my life? *Like* why don't I just kill myself? *Like* actually this is crap city and I'm crap person of the year? Ouch! I feel bad, not about school or teachers or . . . just bad . . . and sad. Probably badder and sadder than I've ever felt in my life.

Maybe I'd better sneak downstairs and take a few puffs of my feel-good friend.

March 29th—Saturday—7:01 a.m.

When Marcie and Bridget and I first talked about doing a little pot we said we'd do it only on weekends. Now our stash is almost gone because *I've* been doing it nearly every day. I'm afraid to tell them. What to do? Mom cut off my allowance for next week because I *told her off* the other night when I was half in, half out. I'm sooo confused and overloaded, both mentally and physically. I wish I had someone to talk to, preferably my idol, Mr. Johnstone. But would even he understand this mess I've gotten myself into?

8:13 A.M.

He would! He might not approve of everything but he'd explain it and give me answers and suggestions and love me. I guess I'm a little short in the love area right now. I wish I had a pet or something to talk to. I used to talk to Jerald, my gerbil, and he'd look at me and listen intently as long as I rubbed his belly. Sometimes he even acted like he knew what I was thinking and feeling. It's nice having someone to talk to even if it's only a little animal like Jerald. I wish Marcie and Bridget didn't live so far away.

8:28 A.M.

I had to sneak in and steal some money out of Mom's purse. I hated to do it. I really did! But I had to. I've got to carry my weight in our three musketeers thing, and tonight we are going to get our supply from

Silver. Thank goodness Mom is going out with her cronies.

8:14 P.M.

I'm scared witless! How could we have been so dumb! Marcie and Bridget and I were out on the balcony, wearing shower caps and in our underwear and we truly thought we had everything covered when *YIKES* we heard Marcie's dad pounding on the door and calling her. Quickly we put out our joint and scrambled inside to put on our clothes, but we weren't fast enough. Her dad opened the front door, tramped through the house, and faced us like the headlight of a locomotive pointed at three frightened deer.

It seemed as if we were stuck in that position for about an hour. Then he said in his army voice that sounded like thunder and lightning and an iceberg all mixed together, "Jennie, I had a feeling the three of you were up to no good when I met your mother at the gas station and she said she was going to a seminar." His eyes bored right through me. After a few seconds he turned to Marcie and Bridget. "Get your clothes on!" he ordered. He turned to me and commanded, "And you, young lady, from now on *you* lock your doors and keep them locked! Anyone could walk in."

"Yes sir," we all said obediently and at attention.

10:01 P.M.

I'm scared silly and lonely. What is Mom going to do when she finds out? And Marcie's dad? He'll

probably send her away to boarding school somewhere and I'll never see her again. And dear, dear
Bridge. I'm sure her parents will *never* let her have
anything to do with me forever.

Marcie's dad's thundering in keeps playing and
replaying itself over and over in my mind! I'm sure
Bridget and Marcie will tell their parents that *I was*
Silver's friend and *I got* the pot and *I* . . . everything.
It's *all* my fault! Every bit of it. Mom's going to hate
me like everything and I don't have the slightest idea
what to do about it. . . .

I just tried to pray but . . .

Now I lay me down to sleep

I pray the Lord my soul to keep.

If I should die before I wake

I pray the Lord my soul to take

doesn't do it! I wonder if the Lord would want me
if I did die? I wish to hell I could. NO! I WISH TO
HEAVEN I COULD!!! Either way, why would the
Lord or anybody want me if even my mother doesn't
want me? She'll be ashamed of me. She'll say nothing
like this has ever happened in her family before. I'm
such a luckless loser! I was the one who got Marcie
and Bridget into the whole mess. Can *they* ever
forgive me? Will they? *Can* Mom? Will she?

In Literature we once had to memorize "Oh death where is thy sting," and I remember thinking it was the dumbest thing I'd ever heard. Now I understand it like it's scripture, whatever that is. Death seems like the pleasant forever *way out* right now.

4:21 A.M.

I'm seriously wondering about . . . you know . . . blowing out my candle, but . . . how would I do it? I'm such a chicken! Hmmmmm.

March 30th—Sunday—6:45 a.m.

WHEN is Marcie's dad going to tell Mom? She thinks I'm sick. I am! Every time the phone rings I about have a heart attack! Sometimes I wish he'd just up and tell her and get it over with.

March 31st—Monday—4:57 p.m.

School was as blah as everything else. Bridget and Marcie are both grounded. We talked for about one minute during lunch period. They told me they couldn't have anything to do with me. At first I thought my heart would break, then they said they can't see each other, either. I guess that makes it a little easier. No it doesn't! But I *don't care*! So there!

9:22 P.M.

I've got to care! If I don't care about myself who will? Dear Mr. Johnstone said once, "If we treat ourselves like we are worth a penny others will value us the same." Thanks, dear, kind, understanding Mr. Johnstone. You've literally saved my life. I WILL NOT THROW MYSELF AWAY OR LET MYSELF BE TREATED AS WORTHLESS! I AM GOING TO:

1. START WORKING IN SCHOOL SO I CAN GET A SCHOLARSHIP FOR A FINE EDUCATION AND BECOME A SOMEONE, EVEN IF MY PARENTS DON'T WANT TO HELP ME.

2. I'M GOING TO START WITH MY FIRST CLASS TOMORROW.

Oh, yes, and I'm going to work on the APPRECIATION THING Bridget and I started light-years ago. I'm going to be respectful and understanding of *everything*! *Positively everything*!

That's going to be really hard, though, because I can't for the life of me figure out the difference between *me using pot and Mom using pills to dull our pain*. Oh, well, I guess some things we can't figure out. But I'll bet Mr. Johnstone could! I know he could! Thoughts of him are very comforting to me.

AND I will *never* use drugs again!

April 2nd—Wednesday—5:46 p.m.

I'm working my little heart out like I said I would.

I went to the library and took out some books so I could catch up on some of the stuff I've been goofing off on, and you know what, today *I'm worth two pennies. And* Marcie's dad *still* hasn't told my mom— maybe he *never* will!

April 3rd—Thursday—9:36 p.m.

Today I found out how come Bridget's parents grounded her. She was afraid Marcie's dad would tell so *she* told. I wish I could but . . . I can't.

Mom's letting me use her new computer anytime I want and it's becoming my true friend. Sometimes when I'm surfing the Net I even find myself talking to it. And you know what else? Mom doesn't seem as much a stranger as she was a while back. She's under a lot of pressure, too. I'll be really glad when I'm old enough to get a job and help her a little with the house expenses and everything. I wonder if Dad helps her, but what good does it do to wonder? I wish like everything I could talk to Mom. Talking is good! I'd even like to talk to her about the drug thing—but I don't dare!

April 4th—Friday—7:12 p.m.

Hockey practice was fun today. Bridget and Marcie and I aren't supposed to be talking to each other (we're all three scared of Marcie's Dad), but in the locker room we did talk a little, and we dreamed up some hand signals: pointer finger *up* means "I miss you"; spread hand *up* means "It will *all* be over soon."

Actually, though, Bridget is grounded for three more weeks and Marcie probably from now on! Thumbs out means "We'll be friends forever," and pinkies touching means "In a few years we'll be in college together and on our own." Those signals make us smile, and it's nice to smile once in a while.

April 5th—Saturday—9:57 p.m.

I've had my head crammed so deeply into a book or a computer lately that I'm hardly in touch with reality, and you know what? That science class that seemed so impossibly hard, well, it's not *that* hard at all now that it's beginning to make sense. In fact, the book *Cells to Nucleus to Genes* is almost like trying to figure out puzzles and it's awesomely, mind-bogglingly fascinating.

April 6th—Sunday—6:10 p.m.

Weekends are long and dull without Bridget and Marcie. Mom and I went to Aunt Meg's and there were a lot of other relatives and friends there, but they were all adults. I feel lonely and alone.

Yesterday I considered for a minute calling Silver, but then I thought it over and quick changed my mind. I'm OUT OF *THERE*!

April 7th—Monday—9:30 p.m.

Since Dad hasn't written to me I decided I'd have

to write to him. I just finished writing a letter. In the morning I'm going to ask Mom to mail it. I really poured out my whole soul to him about how sorry I am that I was such a brat when he was here with us, and how I miss him and wish I had shown him more love and respect. I told him my heart was hungry and homesick for him and that I would never forget him or stop loving him through all of time put together. No one could ever have had a better dad, and I didn't really know how to appreciate him then like I do now. I begged him to please at least write to me or call me sometime. *Now comes the waiting!* I wonder how he'll feel and what he'll say. I do, do, do, do hope he feels like I do and can forgive me and like me a little.

April 8th—Tuesday—7:15 a.m.

I gave Mom my letter to Dad and she didn't seem mad or glad or anything. She just said, "Okay, I'll address it and mail it to him for you," like he wasn't important to her at all anymore. I wonder how that can be, but then I wonder about a lot of things.

April 10th—Thursday—7:14 p.m.

I dashed home from school as fast as I could. Maybe Dad got my letter today. Maybe he'll phone. I wonder what he'll say? Will my letter embarrass him? I hope not! I guess it was pretty silly and childish, though. I hope I didn't make it seem like *he* was to blame for *anything*.

April 12th—Saturday—10:41 p.m.

Dad hasn't phoned or written. I don't understand it. But then I guess I do. Boo hoo to me.

April 13th—Sunday—4:20 p.m.

I am glad I've started on my scholastic journey. It fills in lots of the holes in my life, and besides, it will someday make me a success and famous in whichever field I decide to become an expert in. I think it might be math. I love math! Algebra and geometry are both challenges and a lot more interesting than computer games. It's exciting dealing with points, lines, planes, and solids. Besides, it makes me feel like I'm really on my way to going *where I want to go*! At least in one area of my existence. As for all other things, forget it! I feel like I'm still treading water, going in no particular direction and with a great possibility of going . . . down . . . down . . . down . . . .

That's dumb! I'm just being pessimistic and negative. Maybe I'll be able to see things in a brighter perspective tomorrow.

April 14th—Monday—4:49 p.m.

Today is the day I've been waiting and wishing and dreaming for! I still can't believe it! I really can't. I slouched into my math class in my usual daze, then I felt a touch on my shoulder that was electrifying, and a voice that I'd recognize in my dreams said, "Why so sad, sunshine Jennie?"

I was shocked, and I literally had to restrain myself to keep from turning around and hugging Mr. Johnstone with all my might.

Mr. Johnstone says wonderful self-esteem-building things to everyone in the class. But to me they seem more . . . nourishing, fostering, supportive than to anyone else. But I guess maybe that's just the way I *want* it to be and it isn't that way at all.

Anyway, Mr. Johnstone told the class that Miss Marress is moving permanently to Florida to live with her mother, who is badly crippled—from another stroke. So *he* will be our *forever, full-time* teacher from now on! *Celebration time* started!

The whole class roared and whooped and hollered! I'm surprised that the principal didn't come running.

It's been the most glorious day of my life. I passed papers and felt so smiley inside I thought my face was going to crack. When the bell rang Mr. Johnstone patted everyone's shoulder or arm as they left, but he *squeezed* the back of my neck. It was so . . . so . . . belonging or extrapersonal or . . . maybe just dumb wishful thinking. NO, it *was not* that! Imagine a "beyond perfect" sub-teacher becoming our really, true, forever, permanent guardian and guide!!!!

April 15th—Tuesday—9:30 p.m.

I can't believe how sunny and warm and belonging life is since Mr. Johnstone came back to our class with his stories and jokes. He says nice things to everyone. This is an accelerated class so we don't have any goof-offs, and he's really helping us see that things we once thought of as complicated are really simple. He says, "The concepts we often think are *unfriendly are usually friendly* once we *allow* them *to be our friends*." Isn't that profound and cuddling? Why did I say "cuddling"? Probably because it's true. We want to hold precious things close to our hearts.

My life is good

My life is kind

The greatest life

I'll ever find

And I am nuts

But never mind.

It's great to feel relaxed and cool and happy-silly again. I hope I can stay in this mode for the rest of my existence here on earth.

April 16th—Wednesday—4:37 p.m.

Each day gets better and happier and I *get prettier*. Is that possible or is it just because Mr. Johnstone is making me feel that way? He's my mentor, my teacher, my wise and loyal adviser and friend.

Today when Bridget and Marcie passed me in the hall they bumped into me accidentally on purpose and gave me our pinky sign. They'll both be ungrounded soon, I hope. It will be like a secret, wonderful, mysterious return to some fantasy place.

Neither one of them is in my math class so they can't know the wonders of each day. I can't wait to tell them. But what is there to tell? I guess words can't describe some things.

11:56 P.M.

The phone just rang. In the middle of the night yet. I thought it might be Dad and ran to the kitchen to get the call before Mom picked up the phone in her room. But it was only some guy with a wrong number. Now I'll never be able to go back to sleep.

April 17th—Thursday—4:44 p.m.

Mr. Johnstone passed me a note along with the papers I was to hand out. I slipped it into my jacket pocket close to my heart. It was like I was in grade school. I was so excited I could hardly think straight. I began wondering if I'd done something to upset or displease him, and I could feel my temperature go down below freezing. I wouldn't *knowingly* do anything to upset or hurt Mr. Johnstone for all the money in the world. I hope he knew that. I *almost really* knew he knew it, but you know me, I can be soooooo insecure and wishy-washy sometimes.

Anyway, as soon as the bell rang I dashed into the girls' room, sat down in the first stall I could find, and carefully opened up the note. It said, "I am excited and happy to have you in my class. Your special, beautiful presence makes teaching a joy and a privilege and me a better person." I'm going to put the note in the little box of treasures I've been saving all my life. I guess he does things like this to all the kids but maybe it's not so special to them.

April 18th—Friday—4:49 p.m.

Today I sneaked into Mr. Johnstone's class early and put a big red apple on his desk. It was a silly, childish, dumb little thing, but I couldn't think of anything else to do. My life is sooooooo good!

April 19th—Saturday—10:10 p.m.

Wow! This was a day to remember. Mom woke me up at 8:06 A.M. and said I had a phone call. I usually sleep late on Saturday, so I stumbled to the phone and about dropped over dead when I heard Marcie's dad's voice. He didn't mince any words, he just said, "Jennie, I've talked to your mother and she says you can be at our home at ten A.M. sharp."

"Yes, sir," I answered meekly, and ran into Mom's room to ask her what was going on, half scared he'd told her everything! *But* maybe he hadn't! Maybe *he'd never* tell her! Maybe *I'd* never have to tell her, either!

Mom was sitting up in her bed with her arms

wrapped tightly around her knees, her hair tousled like a little girl's and her eyes so wide they took up half her face. I could tell he *hadn't* told her! "I haven't the slightest . . ." she said with a tiny confused shrug. "General Marchantil just asked if I approved of him talking to you and Bridget and Marcie together about the long-range consequences of actions."

I was bone marrow scared and I felt tears running down my face. Mom reached over and pulled me close beside her. We were both so intimidated by him—her without cause. ME *with* cause! Neither one of us knew what to say, so we didn't say anything. We just hugged and drooled and dripped tears on each other. It sounds wacky but it was nice, like the olden days.

After a little while Mom snuggled closer to me and said, "I don't think he can put you in the brig or court martial you or have you whipped at the post or anything. . . ."

I giggled. "I hope not."

Mom snickered. "I promise I'll bring out the cavalry and come save you if he tries." She saluted. "I know he's just trying to help you in his stiff army way."

The two of us curled up tight on the bed. I love the way my mom smells. She uses a sort of piney woods shampoo and a wildflower after-bath lotion. I've always loved the fragrance! No one else in the whole world smells as sweet and clean and fresh as my mom. If I was blind I'd be like a little seal or kitten before its eyes open, and I could find her anywhere just by her smell.

I am soooo lucky to have my mom for MY MOM! Bridget's mom doesn't have to work and that's good because she's home all the time, but I still wouldn't trade her for my mom for anything. And Marcie's mom, she's . . . great but she's kind of plastic. That's not very nice, and if I were writing with a pencil I'd erase it because I know she really loves Marcie and me and Bridget, too. Any kid in the world would be lucky to have Marcie's or Bridget's mom for a parent; but *my* Mom is especially special! When I finally got around to telling her about us smoking pot and getting caught she understood and loved me anyway. Isn't that wonderful!

I'm sooooooo sorry I've been thinking and writing only bad things about my mom for such a long time. It was not her fault that Dad . . . but back to Marcie's dad. I was worried sick that he would tell the three of us that we could never see each other again, or he'd banish us off to Hell or someplace. Marcie said he can do *almost anything* he's so high in the UNITED STATES GOVERNMENT.

My knees were shaking like castanets as I walked up the long walkway to Marcie's house. Her dad opened the door dressed in all his army finery. He put out his arm to gesture me into the library, where Bridget and Marcie were sitting like two frozen little ducks on a frozen pond. I wondered if everyone could hear my knees bonging with each step I took.

It was really a bizarre experience. Marcie and Bridget and I all had to stand while Marcie's dad asked us if we had considered what we had done and what might have happened. His lecture went on forever, and we were standing at such stiff attention that every muscle and nerve in our bodies were about to disintegrate or calcify or something, at least mine were.

It was a horrible experience but it was a good one, too, in a strange kind of way. None of *us* had a chance to say a word but I knew Marcie and Bridget's minds were racing like mine. Never *once* had we thought about THE CONSEQUENCES OF OUR ACTIONS! He said he'd delayed talking to us or our parents so we would have a chance to *penalize ourselves*!

I really feel guilty, because Mr. Johnstone has told me and our class many, many times about that. I guess most people haven't ever thought about it.

When the lecture was finally over I couldn't believe what I did. I went up to Marcie's dad and offered to shake his hand and thank him. I could feel salty tears running into my mouth and some little part of me thought he might pull his white gloves out of someplace and slap me across the face, but guess what? He knelt down and hugged me, then Marcie and Bridget were in his hug, too, and I even detected tears in his eyes as he told the three of us how precious we were to him and that he HAD to impress us with the harm we had been inviting into our lives.

It was really neat and sweet and I didn't want our hug to ever end, but it did, and he went back to being his stiff, stern self. I guess Marcie and Bridget and I will go back to being our old airhead selves. BUT NOT AS AIRHEADED AS WE USED TO BE!!! Not after today! We promised him that in the future we would always take a time-out to THINK before *each ACTION*!!!

What a wonderful, learning, growing day. It ended with me and Bridget and Marcie happily mall prowling and junk stuffing. Life is back to being awesomely, gloriously normal.

When I told Mom about our experience with Marcie's dad, *she* was *very* understanding. She is so great!

April 21st—Monday—7:32 p.m.

This should rattle your pages. Mr. Johnstone took one look at me in class and said, "What wonderful, amazing thing has happened to turn the sunshine overload on inside you?"

Isn't that almost scary? Imagine him reading my deepest inner feelings. I just smiled because I'm sure he knows exactly what happened—well, maybe not exactly, but sort of. He is like no one I've ever met before in my life: intelligent, kind, compassionate, patient, *clairvoyant*, empathetic, understanding, caring, loving—*I mean loving* in a religious, good, help-all-mankind way. *How I wish* my dad had . . . No! No! No!!!!!!!!!

Things can only ruin my day IF I LET THEM! Mr. Johnstone told us that when Steve Mills was going through a hard period. And Mr. Johnstone is the one person I can believe in unconditionally! I love it when he touches me or squeezes my shoulders. It re-energizes me—*restores me*!

Good night, good, sweet, kind, glorious world. Oh, I have to write the three things I'm thankful for and I'm going to get Marcie and Bridget to start doing it, too.

APPRECIATION THINGS

1. I APPRECIATE MR. JOHNSTONE. HE IS MY HERO.

2. I APPRECIATE BRIDGET. SHE IS MY HEROINE.

3. I APPRECIATE MARCIE AND HER DAD.

SOMETIMES HE'S SCARY BUT MOSTLY HE'S WONDERFUL.

I know I only usually write three things, but tonight I've got to include my mom. I don't know where my head has been the last few months. I've been trying to blame her for everything bad and sad in my life. She's not the pill-head I've made her out to be. She's just overworked and worried and as screwed up about life as I am. Well, maybe not that screwed up, but she's got lots of worries and problems, too, and I've never thought about her side before. I feel sorrow because Dad dumped me, but she must feel *it a thousand times worse*!

They dated when they were in high school and got married when they were in college. I am so self-centered I can hardly believe it! She earns the living and does the shopping and worries about the plumbing and the bills and stuff, and I just complain.

I've got to do some changing in my life, some growing up, some thinking about other people, especially Mom. And I'm going to start doing just that. Right now! Right this very minute!

Mr. Johnstone tells us often, "Your *attitude* determines your altitude," and he is righter than rain, whatever that means. Mom loves all the old sayings that her grandmother used to use, and I love them, too. Even though they don't make much sense, they still feel good; maybe it's a family belonging bonding thing.

April 22nd—Tuesday—9:27 p.m.

I'm walking on air, about a foot off the ground.

Mr. Johnstone asked me if I'd stay a minute after class so I could take some papers down to be photocopied. Of course I said YES! with my heart beating like a maxi-load trip-hammer. I feel *privileged* to do anything for him; he does so much for me and my ego. Well, anyway, after he handed me the papers, he gently stroked my hair and said petting me is like petting a little new kitten just barely opening its beautiful big round eyes to see the world. Isn't that lovely and sweet? My hair is like soft little kitten fur.

I wish I could tell Bridget and Marcie how I feel about Mr. Johnstone, but of course I can't. They wouldn't understand. They *couldn't* unless they had him for a teacher. I am sooooo lucky! I guess I kind of revere him. And that's even hard for me to understand. But someday I'll tell them.

Bridge and I went with Marcie after school to pick up a present for her mom's birthday. We went to practically every shop in the mall before she found the absolutely perfect gift, a sweet pair of house slippers with little hearts on them. We wrapped them in gold paper with a big pastel flowered bow. It was fun.

April 23rd—Wednesday—10:42 p.m.

Every day since Bridge and Marcie got out of house arrest we've been like three Siamese twins. Can there be such a thing as Siamese triplets? We've done our homework together at one house or another every night this week, and we're having a sleep-over at Marcie's. Life is all around as good as it gets! If it were any better I think I'd explode from happiness!

April 24th—Thursday—8:40 p.m.

Last night's sleep-over was the greatest! Our *first one* on a weeknight. Marcie's parents were at some big to-do and the maid was supposed to be looking after us, but she stayed in her room. We had the whole house to ourselves till about midnight, and we pretended to be everyone important since the beginning of time. It was silly and fun and Bridget and I taught Marcie all the dumb things we did when we were little kids. She loved it! She doesn't remember having a *real true* friend her own age till she met us two nutcases. Isn't that the saddest thing ever?

We promised we'd be in bed and *asleep* by ten P.M. but we probably didn't get more than a couple of hours' sleep because we acted like nuts till Marcie's parents got home, then we crept through the house or giggled and whispered about cute boys and our wish lists and stuff.

April 25th—Friday—9:06 p.m.

Marcie's mom went to Washington, D.C., with her dad and the maid is sick, so Marcie is staying with me till late Sunday night. It's really fun and sister-ish. We fought over who would get the shower first and who got the biggest piece of cake. Mom laughed herself silly because she said it was just like her and Aunt Meg when they were our age.

It was wonderful to hear Mom laugh and have fun. I wish that Marcie really was my sister or we could adopt someone so we could be like that all the time. That's a dumb thought! But it's a *good* one.

April 28th—Monday

Mr. Johnstone manages to touch my hair and neck nearly every day. It's our kind of special sign. He is soooo special! Bridget and Marcie think that I've got a crush on him. They don't understand his . . . wonderfulness.

March 29th—Tuesday

Mr. Johnstone came around the corner of the library at lunchtime when Bridget and Marcie and me had our arms around each other and were doing the grapevine dance down the walkway. We were singing and being extremely silly. At first he looked startled, then he almost frowned and quickly turned away.

Why do I feel so guilty? We weren't doing anything wrong. Does he think it wasn't proper? I feel bad about the look of displeasure on Mr. Johnstone's face. I wouldn't upset him for anything.

April 30th—Wednesday—4:32 p.m.

I was a little uncomfortable when I walked into Mr. J's class but then he managed to walk past me while I was putting a book back and he slipped a little something into my shirt pocket.

I was antsy for the rest of the class. He acted like nothing had happened so I tried to act the same but it wasn't easy.

As soon as I could get to the girls' room and into a stall, I unwrapped the package, which was about the

size of my little finger. It was a bottle of Spring's Wild
Rose perfume, and it smelled exactly like wild roses,
clean and mountain-ish and out in the middle of
beauty, peace, and nature. As I put my nose against the
unopened bottle I could see myself on Wild Horse
Ridge looking down at the world . . . free . . .
unfettered . . . *cared about!* The feeling was
wonderful. Mr. *J cares about me!* I'm *sure* he doesn't
do this to everyone—at least I HOPE HE DOESN'T!

May 1st—Thursday—4:29 p.m.

Each day of my life gets better, except that
Bridget's old boyfriend, Brad, is trying to make up
with her. I hope she doesn't do it. I really, truly,
honestly do hope she doesn't. He hurt her so badly
when he dumped her before. I don't know what she'd
do if it happened again.

But maybe Marcie and I are just jealous. Maybe
I'm jealous because I've never *really* had a *REAL*
boyfriend. I've liked a lot of boys but none of them
has ever REALLY gone out of his way for me. But in
my heart I can't stand to see Bridge hurt again. I guess
I feel almost like a mother would feel when her kid
was being used and abused, AND IT'S NOT GOOD!
In fact, it's terrible!

I wonder if I could talk to Mr. J about this. I know
he'd know what to do. Hmmmm, maybe I'll think
on that. I'm trying *not* to think about anything . . .
like . . . *school being out soon* and *me not having
Mr. J to support me.* I've *got* to think about something
else!!!!

10:01 P.M.

I wish I could sleep. It doesn't make sense that I'm so sad and scared about Bridge and yet so happy for her because *she's happy.* I saw her and Brad standing in the hall holding hands and she didn't even see me. She only saw him. I hope that happens to me someday, but I've waited sooooooo long. Why don't any of the guys like me? What's wrong with me—other than I'm flat as a pancake and skinny as a rail, and as personality gifted as a post.

Nobody likes me

Everybody hates me

I'm going out to eat worms.

I remember Bridge and I saying that when we were little tiny kids. I guess I'm just being childish and morbid and negative *again*!!!! What a bad way to go! *I gotta have an attitude overhaul. And nobody can give it to me BUT ME! Mr. J said so!*

He is soooo wise and kind and understanding. Each day when he touches my hair and neck it's like we're bonding a little more. It's even greater than that, it's like I'm becoming more and more part of him by osmosis, part of his gentleness and caring and . . . everything. I wrote him a little thank-you note telling him how much I appreciate the perfume and how much he's changing my life for good. It was really hard to write because I didn't want to be too gushy or childish, and I don't want anyone to think I'm a teacher's pet. I hope someday I'll be able to really talk to him one-on-one without having to feel sneaky about it.

April 3rd—Saturday—7:30 a.m.

I had the weirdest dream. I was the sleeping princess in the fairy-tale castle all covered with vines and brush, and I was trying to wake up but I couldn't. I just kept getting more and more tangled up in my sheet, which seemed like vines in my dream, and I was trying to cry out for help. Then it was like a boarded-up window was being opened. The sunlight exploded through in one of those great spotlights beams like on a parking lot in front of a big store opening. It almost blinded me until I saw that coming through the middle of the beam of light was PRINCE JONATHAN JOHNSTONE. He came to me and gently untangled me, and he was carrying me out to his white steed when the phone rang. It was Marcie wanting to bicycle up to Hangman's Cave. WHAT A CHANGE IN TIME AND SPACE! ME HAVING TO CHOOSE BETWEEN FAIRY LAND AND HANGMAN'S CAVE. Guess I don't have much choice but to take reality. DARN!

8:26 A.M.

I had my bike out and my backpack stuffed with junk food and drinks when Marcie called and said her mom had grounded her because she'd talked back. I was furious and mumbling to myself about what a jerk she was, when Mom passed me in the hall and asked what was wrong.

I don't know what happened to me then because I just started crying and slumped down on the floor. Mom grabbed me like she'd never let me go and whispered over and over again, "It's okay, sweetie. Whatever it is we can handle it." She sniffed, "Together we can, baby. We can, we can, we can."

I started chanting along with her. "We can! We can! We can!"

Suddenly it struck me as absurd that Mom and I were clinging to each other like we were going down with the *Titanic* when I was just mad because Marcie had been grounded. Why didn't Mom tell me, "We can handle it" when Dad left us? I started giggling, then laughing. After a minute Mom started laughing with me. Then we were laughing and crying at the same time. It was like lancing an infected wound. I remember when I'd kept my pus-filled knee a secret from Mom till the day she happened to come into the bathroom as I was stepping out of the shower. I grumbled and yowled all the way to the Emergency Room. Goosh started running out like it was a small volcano. I remember the pain and awfulness running out with it. *Like now!* Isn't that weird? Except that *then* Mom had understood me and loved me. Now she was probably just feeling sorry for me.

My eyes filled with tears. I looked into her face and with surprise saw all the exact same feelings that were sloshing around inside of *me*: love, compassion, belonging, caring, security, foreverness, and *fear*. It was a belonging safe moment I will retain all the days of my life.

Well, after a while we got ourselves together and I told Mom about Marcie chucking me. She grinned and said *she'd like* to ride with me up to Hangman's Cave, if I didn't mind, and that we could go deep inside and sit on the very rock she sat on with her grandpa when he told her the spooky *true story* about the cave. She said *it* like we were there already.

9:59 P.M.

It's been a wonderful, glorious, happy beyond happy day. Mom and I talked and talked and talked! I can't believe *Mom felt that I was closing her out*! Just like *I* felt *she* was closing *me* out! And I was. I hated myself so much it sloshed and spilled and splattered out all over her. Poor, poor dear Mom, trying to contact and communicate with me and *me* always trying to push her away. We never mentioned Dad, but that was because she didn't need to be dumped on *again*, especially by a nerd like me.

After Dad left, I was so busy with my own pity party that I thought *everything* and *everybody* were out to get me, blame me, hate me! I remember as clearly as if it were now, this very minute: Mom was reaching out, and I was pushing her hand away and feeling as if she was as much my enemy as Dad.

May 4th—Sunday—6:21 a.m.

I've been crying for forever thinking about what

a selfish, self-centered, unappreciative, destructive person I've been. I hope that someday God can forgive me. I don't even know what that means . . . but I guess I do, too. I hope I do. I hope what I think is true.

May 5th—Monday—5:14 p.m.

My life is sooooo good I feel like I'm living in a movie. Yesterday Mom and I spent the whole day driving around Sunnyville, going up to the falls and to a farmer's market and art show. We talked and giggled and joked. I know we will be forever together no matter what, and I'll be *taking care of her* when she is old and gray like she took care of me when I was young and dumb.

May 6th—Tuesday—6:45 p.m.

This is really strange. Mr. J saw me and Bridget and Marcie huddled by the front stairs giggling and whispering and he said almost sternly, "Jennie, please meet me in my room as soon as possible."

They laughed about it and made snide remarks about what kind of trouble I was in this time, but it wasn't funny to me. My blood was like slush.

When I got to Mr. J's room he apologized profusely and said he'd been having a headache over his right eye and had distorted vision and he just wondered if I could help him for a few days.

I was elated, as if I were standing in the middle of the brightest sunlight in the world, where a second before I had been choked by clutching darkness. He's a *magician* on top of everything else that's good!

May 7th—Wednesday—8:01 p.m.

Poor, sweet Mr. J. Today he came to school wearing a patch over his right eye. He told us he'd gone to the doctor, and he had something that wasn't serious, only that it might take a while to clear up.

After class he told me he had gotten permission from the principal for me to be his aide until his eye was well—that is, if I could spare the time and wanted to. Did I want to? Do birds poop on your porch? When he said "Till I get *well*," he sounded like a little boy and I felt so sorry I wanted to hug him, but of course I didn't dare.

Mr. J wouldn't let me start today. Again, he said he wanted me to talk to my mother about it first. He's so thoughtful!

May 9th—Friday—6:02 p.m.

Today I worked for Mr. J after school and I've never felt so needed and wanted and important. I am so, so, so, so grateful that he chose *me*! *Why*, when he could have chosen anyone in the whole school, probably the whole town or the whole world? He once said he'd moved around a whole lot. I HOPE HE NEVER, NEVER, NEVER MOVES FROM HERE! I think I'd die if he did. Oh, that's childish! Especially now that I'm an AIDE to the most popular teacher at school.

After the bell rang and the other students had left, Mr. J gently rubbed my shoulders and told me how forever grateful he was for my help. Little did he know how proud and mature it made *me* feel to file and photocopy and help make up interesting, funny tests.

I can't wait for Monday! I *really truly* am going to have trouble waiting for Monday!

9:37 P.M.

Marcie's mom dropped me and Bridget and Marcie at the Pizza Hut and then picked us up after the movie. Bridget sneaked away as soon as Marcie's mom was out of sight and went somewhere with Brad. Marcie and I both wish we had boyfriends. What makes a guy like a girl? We talked about that for a long time and obviously WE DON'T KNOW! If we did know what to do you can bet we'd do it in a second and we'd dump each other mucho pronto like Bridget dumped us. *That* sounds terrible but it's almost surely true.

ANYWAY, I'VE GOT MR. J, AND THAT'S PRETTY WONDERFUL! WONDERFUL ENOUGH FOR ME! I wish I could tell Marcie and Bridget how I feel—but I think they'd laugh and tease me about having a crush on him. I'm sure they would.

May 10th—Saturday

Dull day. Bridget is who knows where, Marcie is out of town with her folks, and Mom is at a seminar.

Poor lonely me

Lonely as can be

I wish that I could see

The road in front of me.

Or do I?

May 11th—Sunday—12:49 a.m.

I don't know what happened yesterday. Marcie and Bridget and I had a big fight on our way to the public library where we were going to help sort books after their big water pipe leak. I have no idea what started the bickering. It just seemed like Bridget was in a bad mood and then Marcie and I got on the *negative* bandwagon, too.

After we'd moved heavy books for a few hours we each went home without speaking.

1:10 P.M.

I think probably Bridget and Brad are having problems again, and she was just brewing in her own frustration until it became contagious and we came down with it, too. Anyway, I hope we'll get well again and make up. We've got to! I don't think I could live without Bridget and Marcie. I'm not sure I'd even want to.

2:20 P.M.

I just called Bridget and we laughed about the whole library thing and guessed we're still spoiled babies. But we still decided to give ourselves gold stars for doing our public duty with the heavy, old library books. Mostly we passed the dry ones up in a line of kids, parents, and old people. It was kind of fun.

2:35 P.M.

I just called Marcie's house pretending I needed an English assignment from her. She said she was just trying to phone me and that it was okay for *forever friends* to sometimes get mad at each other and that we'd be even better friends when we made up. We didn't talk long because she wanted to call Bridget and tell her the same thing. Just as she hung up she told me to wish my mom a happy Mother's Day for her. My body shivered. How could I have forgotten Mother's Day? Television and newspapers and signs have been blaring about it forever! I am soooo selfish and self-centered!

2:40 P.M.

Mom said she'd be home about three and we'd

do something. Why would she ever want to do something, anything, with ME? Her own only daughter who can't even remember to buy her something for Mother's Day. I wonder . . . yes, I will! I'll take the precious little bottle of perfume Mr. Johnstone gave me and go pick a big rose and pull off the petals and then wrap the bottle in the petals and hold the petals with transparent plastic wrap. I saw that on a Martha Stewart program. I hope it will work! It's got to! And Mom will never know how much a *secret part of my life* her present is!

9:58 P.M.

Mom simply loved her present, but what was not to love? We went to dinner at the Regency Hotel, where I pigged out like a starving child from a third-world country, then we took in a movie. It was a lovely, lovely Mother's Day for both of us, and dear Mr. J (and his present) was a part of it; that just made everything even lovelier.

May 12th—Monday—8:12 p.m.

I can't believe how comforting and safe it is to work with Mr. J. I feel like it's the only place in the world where *I can do no wrong*! He's always complimenting me and massaging my shoulders when I get tense and . . . well, actually today we really didn't do much . . . in fact, any work at all! We just passed papers back and forth to each other and laughed and talked. He keeps asking me about every little detail in my life and wants to help me get everything straightened out so I can avoid the pitfalls that so many kids stumble into. I actually told him about the Mom-Dad thing and he was so understanding that I wanted to . . . I don't know what . . . I just wanted to show him my physical appreciation for all he was doing for me. I will forever be indebted to him for helping me get through this rugged fourteenth year of my life.

The hour and fifteen minutes I was with him ended in what seemed like a minute.

Sweet dreams to me

And what I'll be

It's up to me

And we shall see.

I'm even beginning to appreciate English and Mrs. Thurber's poetry concepts more. Words really can paint pictures. Maybe someday I'll write a poem that will convey to Mr. J exactly how much I appreciate him, or would that be silly?

9:01 P.M.

I haven't even let myself believe that *the day after tomorrow* will be the last day of school, and I may never see Mr. J again! I wonder if I'll become the old no-confidence, no-personality, no-possibilities non-person I used to be? It's scary and I *won't* let myself think of it anymore. It's like I go from being a solid substance around him to being a *liquid* when I'm not. That's stupid . . . but it's true! What am I ever, ever, ever going to do over the long, long, long, long summer without Mr. J?

May 19th—Monday—8:27 p.m.

Spent some time at the public library repairing children's books. Mom's friend is the librarian. It's kind of snurf work in a dungeon-like little room with no windows. I don't think I could handle it for a long period of time.

Later I played baseball in the park with some kids from school, but no one I feel completely comfortable with. Silver was there, but she scares me a little. She *fascinates* me, too, though. Probably because she's so worldly and everything but . . . I don't know . . . I kind of keep looking over my shoulder when I'm with her. That's odd, isn't it? I guess I just want a safe person to hold my hand and take me places and do things for me.

May 20th—Tuesday—5:32 p.m.

Mom came home with the best news in the world! She's traded vacation times with, I can't remember who, and we're going to *Yellowstone Park*! Her friend had all the reservations and stuff, and then her husband broke his leg in some crazy kind of accident. Isn't that wonderful! Well . . . *wonderful for us*; probably not so wonderful for them! Wow! I've *always*, all my life, wanted to go to Yellowstone Park! We leave in two days.

June 1st—Sunday

Sorry I didn't take you with me, diary, but we were in such a mad dash to get off that I'm lucky to have remembered my head. Anyway, there were geysers and bears and colored pools hot enough to boil eggs in, and buffalo and rainbow-hued mountains and horseback riding through meadows that were so beautiful and fragrant that Mom and I wanted to stay there forever. It was almost like a fantasy. And the *lodge*, all made of huge logs, was like unbelievable. I wish everyone in the whole world could go to Yellowstone National Park at least once. I wish I could go a million times! My bed is calling me. I'm so blissfully tired I can barely hold up my pencil. Nite.

June 2nd—Monday—6:47 p.m.

Dull day. Mom had to go back to work and I had to put away all the junk we brought home. Bummer!

June 3rd—Tuesday—9:10 p.m.

Even duller day. Bigger, badder bummer!

June 4th—Wednesday—9:22 a.m.

It's the most awesomely amazing moment of my life! I was sitting here bored out of my skull, wishing SOMETHING, *ANYTHING* would happen and *guess what*? The phone rang and it was—*guess who—Mr. Jonathan Johnstone!* And *guess what?* He's going to teach summer school and he wants me to be his aide again!!!!!!! Glory hallelujah! The sky is falling up! Mr. J will be teaching a younger class and the kids have problems so he'll need a lot of assistance. ME! AN ASSISTANT to kids with dyslexia and attention deficit disorders and conduct disorders! All the lights in the firmament have turned on full power.

Mr. J says *we'll* have only sixteen kids because they need more one-to-one help. But imagine him saying WE will be teaching them! I'm pinching myself black-and-blue because I still can't believe it!

June 5th—Thursday—6:02 a.m.

Last night Mom and I talked for a long, long time. I told her how sad I was because Marcie had left and how lonely I was going to be when Bridget left to spend most of the summer with her Auntie Jane in Texas, who just had triplets! Imagine three babies to take care of at one time! Bridget didn't really want to go because of Brad. Of course, I didn't tell Mom that. But when I told Mom about Mr. Johnstone asking me to be his AIDE again for two hours on Mondays, Wednesdays, and Fridays, she was almost as delighted as I was. She said she thought it would be good for me and certainly good for the kids, having someone just a little bit older to help them. She said she'd been a volunteer, too, when she was my age, first at the library and later as a Candy Striper at the First Methodist Hospital. She said they wore pink striped aprons, like candy canes, and took flowers and books and stuff to people who were sick. That sounds like fun, and if I wasn't privileged to work with Mr. Johnstone I think I'd try it.

10:06 P.M.

After we'd both gone to bed I remembered that I rarely tell Mom how much I appreciate her and what she does for me. I went to her room and snuggled up in bed beside her and told her what she really, truly means to me and how sorry I am that sometimes I treat her like dirt.

She cried, and then I cried. We talked about love and respect and stuff. I wanted like anything to bring Mr. J into our conversation but for some reason it didn't seem right. This was *our* time and we've had so little of it I didn't want to share a second.

Mom was like the old Mom, and I felt sheltered and good inside until I walked past her room a few minutes later to go to the bathroom and she was taking the pills I hated, hated! HATED! I wanted to go in after she was asleep and flush them down the toilet . . . but she'd just get more. I wonder, is she *REALLY ADDICTED* AND SHE CAN'T STOP?

Oh, crap! How can one minute seem so heavenly and the next seem so hellish?

Maybe I'll talk to Mr. J about it. I trust him more than I trust anyone else, *especially her doctor!* He's the one who loads her up till she's not herself. It's not Mom's fault. He's the one I *ought* to hate, AND I *DO HATE* him! And Dad?

I won't let myself think of him. I'll think of nice, kind, wise Mr. J and what he'd do; that will help me go to sleep. Dear, dear Mr. J. He's the only one in the world who keeps me from exploding and splattering all over the ceiling.

June 7th—Saturday—7:03 a.m.

Will Wednesday ever come? Wednesday is when I see Mr. Johnstone and *our* students. I can't wait! I can't, I can't . . . but I guess I *can*. I don't have much choice.

10:46 P.M.

Mom and I drove out to see Aunt Meg and Uncle Harry. Meg was feeling and acting like her old self. She looked beautiful and was wonderful and funny to Mom and me and especially to Uncle Harry. They seemed as much in love as two young kids . . . no, not kids—affectionate, appreciative young adults, and they aren't even young. It was lovely to see them with their arms around each other. That's the way love and life should be, could be, IF PEOPLE ONLY CARED ENOUGH AND TRIED HARDER. I won't let myself think of Mom and Dad together . . . that still brings back a kind of pain that isn't either mental or physical, and yet it is worse than both of them put together.

Anyway, Mom says Aunt Meg stopped drinking

some weeks ago and everybody's so happy they can hardly stand it. I wish we lived closer to them. Aunt Meg is sooooo sweet and special when she's not drinking, and Uncle Harry is quiet but he's . . . everything I wish Dad was. Dad was Uncle Harry's best man when he and Aunt Meg were married. I remember a picture we had of their wedding. Uncle Harry wrote across the front, "My Best Man and My Best Friend. Forever!" What a crock. Uncle Harry the dude in the white hat and Dad . . . forget it! *I wish I could!*

June 8th—Sunday—4:43 p.m.

Today Mom and I went to the lake early and fed the ducks and geese and swans. It was quiet and restful—well, maybe not quiet—with all the bird families, but it was just us and them. Mom saw one beautiful swan with a silly little baby swan floating along behind her. It kept almost running into its mom and not swimming quite straight and Mom started laughing and said they were US. We plopped down on the grass and sat with our arms around each other. I LOVE her sooooo much and she is so kind and good and helpful to me! I don't know what I'd do without her and I wouldn't trade her for any other mom in the world. Sometimes I'm so disrespectful to her. I don't know how she stands me . . . and obviously Dad couldn't!

Well, to hell with that! I don't need him and he doesn't need me. So what? Who cares?

Come on, kid! Get yourself together. Mom and

Mr. J both say I can't let unimportant things ruin my life. They're right, and Dad is probably the *MOST UNIMPORTANT* THING IN CREATION!

Hey, I just noticed I put Mr. J and Mom in the same thought pattern. That's nice. It makes me feel good and like . . . wanted and protected on both sides of me.

Oh, I almost forgot to write that Mom and I had brunch on the riverboat that the Smothers have fixed up with six really little tables. It was fun and the food was tasty, and Mr. Smothers played his banjo and sang old country folk songs while his wife smiled and served and sometimes sang with him. Their teenage son drove the boat for a while, then Mr. Smothers took over and Josh played his guitar and sang country and bluegrass. He's supercute. He couldn't see me from dog doo but then he didn't look at anyone else, either. He was *really* shy!

After we'd eaten, Mrs. Smothers drove the boat and Josh and his dad played together. It was funny and happy, and we all felt like family before we docked. Mom called me her "little sweet swan" all the way home and it was a lovely day that sped by too fast.

11:10 P.M.

I just woke up and can't go back to sleep—no matter what I do. Time has stopped dead in its tracks. Won't this night evvvvvvvvvvvveeerrrrrrrrrrrrrr end?

11:32 P.M.

In four mornings, if mornings ever come, I will be teaching with Mr. J. I truly think I will literally detonate before then!!! I CAN *NOT* WAIT! Wednesday, please come!

June 9th—Monday—7:45 a.m.

I don't know how I could have slept late when I'm so excited about Wednesday and today!

2:32 P.M.

I've been at the library all morning, but this time I didn't just do repairs on books, I was asked to help two little Latina girls with their reading. At first the girls, seven and eight years old, could hardly read at all. We started with the simplest of all books: "The boy saw a cat. The boy saw a dog. The boy saw a pig," etc. It wasn't dull, though. In fact, it was almost magic with us making whispery animal sounds to each other between pages as the wiggly squiggle lines began to represent sounds. Then we went back to the beginning, and first Evenita, then Marie, read the whole book to the end without a mistake. They were so proud! Next we read two simple phonics books.

We were all curled up together on a beanbag chair and I was reading *The Little Lost Angel*, when Miss Haynes came over and told us it was almost noon. We couldn't believe three hours had passed so quickly.

Both Evenita and Marie begged me to come teach them to read next Saturday. I felt like I was Mr. Johnstone. Someone loved me, admired me, needed me, and appreciated me. Wow de dow! What a feeling of importance! Now I'll have to choose between being a librarian and a teacher when I grow up.

I don't know which would give me more satisfaction and pride in myself. Yawn. I guess choices will have to wait.

June 10th—Tuesday—3:10 p.m.

I can't imagine what I *used to do* during my long summer vacations! I'm bored spitless. I am so, so, so, so grateful that I have Mr. J to work with on Monday, Wednesday, and Friday, and Evenita and Marie to work with on Saturday. How lucky, lucky, lucky I am and how blessed, blessed, blessed.

This is really weird but I feel like my life is just *now* beginning! Is that strange or what?

June 11th—Wednesday—4:06 p.m.

What a wonderful day I've had—well, two hours of a wonderful day! I only get to work from one to three, and the students are all little kids in the fourth grade. Our room is in one of the bungalows behind the school, since the grade school is being renovated. I can't believe how young and immature they are. Most of them have troubles I've never seen before. Jed keeps twitching, and occasionally strange noises come

out of him that he can't control. Amy has severe
attention disorder. It seems strange because she's an
absolutely breathtakingly beautiful child. Lacy and the
others are almost constant challenges and they do
almost need a one-to-one teacher . . . OR *AN
INSPIRED AND INSPIRING MR. J.*

Mr. J is sooooo wise. He says to always start the
kids with something that is *below* their level. For some
of them it's pretty low, but doing it that way makes
them feel better about themselves and their ability.
Isn't that a brilliant caring concept? Oh, also some of
the kids are so bright in some ways it's amazing, and
even scary.

Mrs. Dawson—she's old and big and fat—works
with Mr. J three hours in the mornings. She's an aide,
too. She says, "We're all three just trying to find our
way into the hearts and minds" of the kids.

She's really patient and comfortable to be around.
That should help all sixteen of our little out-of-sync
students. At least I hope it does. I'm trying very hard
to be patient and kind, too! It's *not* easy!

Mr. J didn't have much time for me today but
that's all right because his students need him more
than I do.

Once, though, when the kids were out for recess,
he petted my hair softly and said he'd "really, really
missed me." I thought my heart was going to explode,
I felt so good, but just then Mr. J had to dash out to the
school yard to help Mrs. Dawson stop a fight.

Occasionally, Mr. J has Mrs. Dawson take one kid
at a time to the arbor to study. That's the only time we
have alone together, in the hall, and it seems like it's
just for a second.

June 13th—Friday—9:47 p.m.

I can't believe this! Marcie's moving to D.C. on Thursday. Her parents actually thought it would be *less* traumatic if they didn't let her know in advance. They just told her this morning, and she's been a basket case all day.

When she told Bridget and me we were both just one tear away from making fools of ourselves. I'm going to miss her like crazy, but I'm glad it isn't Bridget who's going.

I wonder if life is as confusing to everyone as it is to me. When school lets out it's like everything and everyone *disappears*, at least it seems that way this year.

June 17th—Tuesday—10:31 p.m.

Marcie's gone and Bridget's out somewhere with Brad and his buddies. I feel so alone. Mom and I went shopping and mall hopping . . . and I love her but . . . I don't know . . . somehow I seem like only half a person.

June 18th—Wednesday—9:59 p.m.

Sorry I misplaced you for a week. I looked all over because there were millions of glorious things I wanted to write but, oh well, *I know* what they are. I live for Mondays, Wednesdays, and Fridays. Mr. J is my honored therapist. He thought at one time that he would be a psychologist and took *lots* of classes. He would have been great, too. No matter how low I feel when I come to help him I leave feeling like the luckiest, happiest girl in the world. I'm almost afraid to say or write the words, but I really do think that he's becoming MY BOYFRIEND. I WISH! I know he's a lot older than I and I've never had a real boyfriend before, but I feel so wanted and appreciated and . . . loved when I'm with him. I just know he feels like I do, too, because each day he finds some little second to hug me or kiss me on the top of my head or something. I'd love to share these beautiful, wonderful things with someone but they're almost too sacred to share even with Bridget and they're hard to hide from Mrs. Dawson when she's around. Mr. Johnstone asked me to call him J.J. when we're alone. He doesn't think I should tell *anyone*, absolutely *NO ONE*, about our "friendship." He thinks they might not understand and then he'd get fired and have to move away. I couldn't stand that. I really COULD NOT! So I'll never, ever, never tell *anyone* under the sun! That's really, really hard. He asked me to carefully destroy the notes he writes me, too—*but I cannot do that!* They are too precious to me. I keep them *locked* away in my treasure chest. He will be glad someday I did!

June 20th—Friday—7:02 p.m.

Wonderful, amazing Friday. J.J. and I sat for an hour after school just writing notes back and forth across his desk like we were correcting papers. It felt kind of amazing and exciting, too. Imagine a teacher and a kid writing notes to each other and being every minute watchful of someone walking by the open door. It was kind of like a mystery game or something.

At first the notes we passed were silly, like, "I really like you," then "*I* really like *you* more than *you* like *me*." After a while they slowly started escalating until I began to feel like I was blushing inside. About that time the janitor banged close by with his cleaning stuff and J.J. got all professional again.

June 21st—Saturday—9:01 a.m.

Can you believe *this* is the day Mom would pick for us to go to Aunt Meg's and Uncle Harry's? I said I'd go because there was nothing else to do. Evenita and Marie are sick. Then at 8:55 J.J. called and asked if I wanted to meet him in the park "accidentally." I wanted to so much I could taste it but I was sure Mom would be suspicious, so I had to tell him about her plans. He seemed kind of sad and said maybe we could do it another Saturday, but not to let *anyone* know about it, especially not my mom or my immature friends. He's always telling *me* how emotionally and mentally mature I am and it makes me feel good, good, good!

I love Bridget and know that even as my precious sister-friend she *is* kind of an *immature blabbermouth*. She wouldn't mean to hurt J.J. and especially not me but . . . well, it's hard to keep an awesome secret like this. Even I have trouble! It might actually be better and nicer to keep it because then *nobody* knows but us! A sacred secret! Wow! Not being able to talk about *it* doesn't mean I can't *THINK ABOUT IT ALL THE TIME*!!

June 24th—Tuesday—4:21 p.m.

J.J. kissed me on the cheek and nibbled on my ear for one second after the kids went to recess. When? Where? Are we ever going to be alone?

June 25th—Wednesday—7:22 p.m.

I think I'm flattered but a little annoyed, too. After class J.J. pulled me behind the door and gave me a quick hard hug, a hug so hard it really hurt, *but hurt good!* Then he whispered that he had "loved" me from the first minute he had laid eyes on me. That I was the "sweetest, dearest little thing that had ever come into his life" and it was like we were fated to meet. Then some squirrely little kid came back to pick up the jacket he'd forgotten. I wanted to beat his brains out, but I remembered: If it weren't for him and his classmates I wouldn't even be here with the forever future light and joy of my life. Every drop of liquid in me became INSTANTLY CARBONATED!

June 26th—Thursday—6:32 p.m.

This afternoon, after school, J.J. and I met "accidentally on purpose" at Apple Annie's Bakery, in a little room on the side where people can eat desserts. We didn't touch, and I'm thinking now that *my hair* and *shoulder* and *back* and *hands* felt lonely for his stroke. I often wonder how I will feel when he finally *really* kisses me.

J.J. tells me such wonderful things about myself

that I sometimes wonder if he can possibly be really talking about skinny, dumb, childish me.

He's asked me if I've ever had a "boyfriend," saying he didn't think he could stand it if any of the "handsy, grabby, testosterone-propelled, pimple-faced little male twits" at school had ever touched any parts of my body that were "sacredly mine."

I didn't mean to laugh but I couldn't stop an embarrassed giggle from popping out. Then he giggled with me. I knew *he knew* by my embarrassed look and red face that I was repelled by boys I know. Even though I have to admit to myself—but never to him, of course—that Bridget and Marcie and I used to spend most of our time *talking* about boys and wondering about . . . well . . . everything!!!!!

A big guy came into the bakery and J.J. immediately jumped up and acted like he knew my Mom. Then he left.

That was strange, but I guess he had to do it. Maybe the man was on the school board or something.

June 27th—Friday—9:40 p.m.

I have never had such a glorious, educational, happy day in all my life. J.J. slipped a note on top of the papers I was to hand out, and I shivered all through class waiting to read it. When I got into the girls' room I opened it with trembling hands.

J.J. was asking me to go to the library after school and pretend to be deeply involved in looking something up until I had missed my bus, then I'd run out and he'd come by and offer me a ride home. Isn't he the cleverest?

I can't believe his car. It's a shiny black convertible Mustang that looks like brand-new, but it isn't. Anyway, he said sometime we'd go for a drive up the canyon with the top down. Isn't that exciting?

On the way home J.J. pulled into a little dead-end alley, and he hugged me so tenderly and gently I felt like I was melting *and* when he kissed me my whole body seemed to be floating. It wasn't a tongue kiss (which I've always wondered about); it was just . . . little nibbly kisses. Then he stopped and asked me about every detail of how I felt. I truly *wanted* to say that I wanted *more* hugging and kissing but he ran his fingers through my hair, piling it on the top of my head, and said he guessed I'd had my lesson for the day.

"Did I pass?" I asked mischievously.

He kissed me again as he started the car. "With an A-plus-plus-plus-plus-plus," he said. Then he grinned.

Oh, yeah! I forgot to tell you that J.J. had put on the bottom of the note that I was to tear it up into little tiny pieces and throw it away as soon as possible, but I can't! I really, really tried to, but I can't! It's too special! It's a part of *HIM* and *ME*! Someday he'll be happy that I lovingly saved all of his notes with the rest of the priceless treasures I've saved so far through my life. They'll be tucked away in my little combination-locked treasure box.

June 28th—Saturday—11:04 p.m.

Bridge and I went to a school play together (she and Brad are having a tiff again). They are *so childish*! He wanted to go to a basketball game with the guys and she wanted him to go to the play. Neither one of them *cared* enough about the other to do what *they* wanted to do! I really think I'm IN LOVE with J.J. because in a minute I'd choose to do what *he wanted* to do, be where *he wanted* to be . . . but maybe not . . . it's just that we have so little time together that . . . I dunno. . . . Anyway, Bridge is sleeping over and she's asleep. *I'm* as wide awake as can be. I wish I could talk to her about J.J. She knows I'm holding something back, but *he* made me *promise* that I would never, never say anything to ANYBODY about us. *ANYBODY!* EVER! At least not for a while. Oh, I tell her some things, but when she starts teasing me about having a "thing" for him, I force myself to pull back. It's not easy!!!

June 29th—Sunday—10:02 p.m.

Long, boring day.

June 30th—Monday—4:46 p.m.

I had a terrible, awful day at school! Long, long, long and lonely! J.J.'s note (he leaves me one nearly every day) said he had a staff meeting after school so *maybe* we could meet Tuesday or Wednesday. Maybe? I don't think I can stand it!!! Evenita and Marie have moved to another part of town. I miss them. I felt complete and capable and important when I was teaching them.

5:21 P.M.

Mom brought in the mail and guess what? A letter from Marcie. Here I was feeling so sorry for myself I wanted to cry or yell or tear something up and then I read how she is in a stuffy private summer school with no friends and her parents so "socially busy" she hardly ever sees them. She must have really been feeling bottomed out when she wrote because her letter was five pages long and mostly about the good old days when she was here with Bridge and me and we were going about doing our triplet silly airhead things. We really did have a lot of fun together! I'll be glad when she's back.

July 1st—Tuesday—6:59 p.m.

Mom and I just had the biggest quarrel of the century. She's made plans for us to go away for the weekend, from Friday noon till Sunday night. Actually, she has to attend a conference and I'll be sitting alone in the hotel bored out of my skin and longing to be home. Why can't I stay here?

How can Mom treat me like such a baby? J.J. says I'm really an important part of the world. She thinks I'm unimportant! I really am helping J.J. with the kids at summer school. They need all the one-to-one help they can get. It's not fair! I'm so mad I wish I could . . . I don't know what. I'm glad I don't know *what*, because I know it wouldn't be acceptable behavior in any way, shape, or form.

If Bridget's family wasn't on vacation I could

probably go stay with them, but they're gone. Maybe I can go stay with Silver . . . ummmm . . . I guess I just better hunker down and do the old slave thing.

At times like this I feel that kids really are slaves in a way.

10:20 P.M.

I'm such a spoiled brat. Mom isn't going because she wants to! Who do I think makes the money to put food on the table and makes the house payment and pays the gas and light bill and on and on? *NOT* dumb self-centered *me*. I'm the taker, *not* the giver. I'm the negative influence, *not* the positive . . . whatever.

10:31 P.M.

I felt so sorry and ashamed of myself for my terrible two-year-old-type tirade to Mom I slithered into her bedroom and tearfully apologized.

She reached up and pulled me down beside her and we cried and then giggled and laughed together about how mixed up we both get sometimes and how easy it is to feed each other's fears.

I love my dear, dear, dear, dear mom. How lucky I am to have her! What would I ever, EVER do without her? I promised with all my heart that I will *never* be disrespectful and rude to her again. Her sweet tears washed my pains away and we are one again as we always will be and always should be.

July 2nd—Wednesday—4:49 p.m.

Rotten day. J.J. had a dental appointment right after school so I barely got a hug and a nibble on my neck.

July 3rd—Thursday—5:37 p.m.

I was supposed to meet J.J. in the alley but he didn't come. I waited for almost an hour till it started getting spooky. I wonder what could have happened to him. Did he have an accident? Is he in a hospital? What if he's dead?

6:30 P.M.

Just as my heart was literally beginning to break (I could feel it cracking on the edges and pulverizing) the phone rang. I jumped up so fast I tripped over the rug and the blood sloshing in my ears made it hard to hear.

When I recognized J.J.'s voice my words tumbled out all over each other: "Where are you? Are you all right? What happened? I've been sick with worry—"

J.J. had to interrupt and tell me that he'd had car trouble at the corner of Spring and Vine Streets and that he'd barely been able to get to a garage; actually, he'd finally had to get a tow truck to take him the last few blocks.

He was soooooooo sorry he'd worried me and I was soooooooo sorry I'd blubbered on him that we wound up laughing, and we talked on the phone for almost an hour before Mom came in. Thank goodness she'd had a late client.

9:14 P.M.

I'm lying here in bed, writing, trying not to forget one single word of what J.J. said to me. He told me how precious I am in his life and how *I* make *him* a stronger, better person with my "blossoming beauty and sweetness and gentle, uncontaminated-by-worldly-things presence." Isn't that the most beautiful phrase ever uttered? It's turned on in my mind like a brilliant Las Vegas neon sign. But I don't deserve it. I truly know I don't. He has no idea what a slimeball mentality I often have, and how crude and rude I sometimes am to my mom and how much I hate my dad's guts.

I'm shivering, thinking about how disgusted he would feel if he knew the real me. I'VE SIMPLY GOT TO CHANGE MY WHOLE *ATTITUDINAL SET* (his phrase) AND I CAN! I WILL! I *WILL* START THIS VERY MINUTE.

I will live in the shadow of his greatness and goodness and let it rub off on me until I become just like him. That's wishful dreaming—but at least I can become *more* tolerant and empathetic and compassionate and long-suffering and forgiving and everything else that's good, LIKE HE IS! Would that everyone had such an awesome *exemplar*. I've never known how to use that word before! But it's perfect for now. And you know what the most amazing thing of all about our conversation was? He told me that he is actually *very shy*! That it is difficult for him to meet people and that he's mostly uncomfortable around them, that he has to try very hard to appear outgoing around . . . get this . . . *everybody but me!* That *I* make *him* feel confident and self-worthy.

Oh, special, special day that he came into my life and I into his! *Two really star-crossed lovers.* Well . . . not really lovers, but I guess neither one of us really felt *complete* until we met. I'd never known what was lacking in my existence before. Now I know! It was him!

He wants me to call him every night after my mom has gone to sleep, since we can't seem to find any time to be alone at school and his car will be in the garage for about a week.

July 4th—Friday—holiday—no school—8:16 a.m.

J.J.'s gone to spend the weekend with some friends so I won't get to even talk to him for THREE WHOLE DAYS! What a lonely, endless time that is going to be. I miss him already, and I'm jealous as . . . I won't say it, but I am *that* jealous. He said his friends were just two old men but I'm thinking . . . that's lame . . . he's entitled to some life out of my orbit, isn't he? I hate to say this but he wouldn't have even one minute away from me if I had my way. He's the only one in the world who makes me feel like a princess, and perfect, and beautiful, and filled with talents and gifts and possibilities and . . . oh, crap, Mom's yelling at me to answer the phone because she's in the shower.

8:59 A.M.

Mrs. Matterly, a lady who works with Mom, just invited us over to their house for a barbecue and to watch the fireworks in the stadium. She said they live in Rolling Hills and the fireworks are spectacular from there. Guess it will be better than just vegetating here.

10:32 P.M.

Just got back from the Matterlys'. It was fun and delicious and spectacular. They've got three kids and what appears to be a perfect marriage. Ron is fifteen. He's kind of cute and he's really fun to play volleyball with, especially if you're on *his* side, which I was. Ron and Tuila, his eight-year-old sister (who didn't count), and his dad, and I were on Ron's team and Mrs. Matterly and Mom and bawl-baby-Katie were on the other one. I didn't know Mom was such a pro, and Mrs. Matterly was even better. Fourteen-year-old Katie was more a handicap than anything else. She bawled when she broke a fingernail and accused Ron of hitting the ball twice, which hc didn't! What an attitude. She needs Mr. J's reinforcement techniques as much as the socially handicapped kids in our summer school session. I feel sorry for her parents. She's really pretty on the outside but inside . . . nada . . . zip . . . yuck.

Anyway, I had a really good timc . . . SUR-PRISE . . . for some reason Ron and I felt very comfortable around each other from the start, like we'd known each other forever. We sat on a pile of big rocks overlooking the stadium and talked about sports. He loves hockey, too, and felt like someone had died in his family when they closed down the Ice Palace, much the way I did. And he likes to volunteer, too, and has had some really interesting experiences working with kids who have birth defects. It was a lovely, normal-family kind of day. One that made me realize how much I was missing in my life. I wanted to talk to Ron about the loneliness I suffered for my dad but that would have been dumb. Something told me he would understand, but I couldn't bring myself to do it, even though I vividly remembered the cleansing, garbage-unloading feelings I've had after I've talked to Bridget or Marcie or Mr. J or my mom.

July 5th—Saturday—9:22 p.m.

Ron and I met on our bikes and rode up to Piney Cove, then we went as far as we could go up on the bike trail, but since we don't have mountain bikes we had to give up at the second ridge. Now both of us want mountain bikes next Christmas. We laughed and talked a lot. He's more like a cousin or something than anything else. I'll probably never see him again after tomorrow, when we are going to try to bike up to Crater Lake. Our parents would kill us if they knew, so we won't tell them.

July 6th—Sunday—10:32 p.m.

I didn't know it was possible to be as tired as I am. Every corpuscle and cell and nerve and ligament and muscle in my body is screaming. I told myself I had to keep up with Ron, and he was probably saying the same thing about me. I took a hot bath and stayed there till my hands were water wrinkled but I still ache. I wonder if I'll even be able to walk tomorrow.

I've GOT TO! Working with J.J. is my absolute destiny!

I guess I'll never see Ron again. He phoned but I don't think J.J. would like it if . . . It's a mixed up world.

July 7th—Monday—7:31 p.m.

J.J. says he was as excited to see me as I was to see him after the long weekend, he is just able to hide his feelings better. We both got to school a little early and he hugged me and hugged me and nibbled at my face and ears till we heard kids yelling and scrambling toward our classroom door, then he gave me a last hard, really hard, bite on my ear and handed me a stack of papers.

Lee Ray's father came to see Mr. J after school so I didn't even get to say good-bye, but I found a note in my backpack. It said to meet him in OUR ALLEY.

I pretended to miss the bus, then walked the three blocks from school and met J.J. His car was fixed early. We sat in our private wonderful little dead-end alley for a while, then he asked me if I'd feel comfortable stopping at a pay phone and calling my mom to tell her I was at the library or the mall or somewhere and I'd be home a little late. It was obvious that *he felt uncomfortable* asking me to lie! He's such a sweet, compassionate, understanding, ethical person! But sometimes *we all have* to do things we don't particularly *want* to do. I know he didn't want me to lie to my mom. I would hate to have him know that *I* really don't *care* that much about the lying. I know I *should*, but we have sooooo little time together and each second is sooooo precious to both of us! I think she'd understand. NO! I KNOW SHE WOULD *NOT* UNDERSTAND! Maybe in a little while I can have J.J. over to our house for dinner or something and she can find out how wonderful he is to me. BUT NOT NOW! Definitely not now!

After I'd called, we drove up to a little spot at Piney Cove and J.J. hugged me and kissed me, and for the first time he told me sincerely that he loved me with all his heart and soul. That he knew from the first moment he saw me that I would be someone very special in his life. Then he pulled away and told me that if I felt I was too young to become involved with him he would understand, but he felt we were meant for each other regardless of our age difference.

I couldn't hold back my tears as I swore my love to him and told him I felt the same way he did.

I was soooo filled with new emotions and joy that I didn't want the afternoon to ever end, but, like all good things, it did! Quite suddenly he pushed me away and said it was time for him to take me home.

I'm embarrassed to tell even you this, diary, but I really wanted him not to stop. His touch and his kiss were ethereal (if that means what I think it means), and I didn't want him to stop, ever, ever, ever!

When he let me off a couple of blocks from my house I had to fight myself to keep from begging him to let me stay. Of course *I didn't*! But I still wanted to!

10:27 P.M.

Very soon the first SUMMER SCHOOL SESSION will be over. I don't know how I'm going to handle that. I truly don't! Being with J.J. for three days a week has been like . . . like what keeps me alive! I haven't allowed myself to think about what now but I *must,* and it's excruciatingly painful! J.J. hasn't said anything about it. Why hasn't he? Can he possibly be as mixed up as I am? I hope not! He's the brilliant older one who can handle all things so I don't need to worry. Right? Right!

I am so grateful I have someone like him in my life that I can trust completely, ABSOLUTELY, UNCONDITIONALLY! It makes me feel *safe* and *belonging* and *protected*! He's right! I couldn't trust some silly little zit-faced boy like I trust him! I trust him with my complete everything! I had no idea LOVE could be like this. It is beyond verbalization totally.

Ron has phoned a couple of times, but I can't feel good about being his *friend* when I'm J.J.'s . . . I don't know what.

July 8th—Tuesday—8:45 p.m.

J.J. was so busy today that we hardly had time to speak. And the kids were either hyper or so moody that my two hours seemed to last forever, and yet they passed in what seemed a minute.

It was almost time to leave when J.J. slipped a note into my hand. It said, "Call your mother. Tell her you missed the bus and meet me in our alley."

We only had a few minutes there because he had an appointment. I wanted to ask him who it was with but of course I didn't dare. I guess I'm even jealous of his dentist, if it was his dentist. Anyway, he said to call him tonight after Mom went to bed. I wonder if she will ever go to bed. She's watching a dumb, dumb movie on TV.

10:30 P.M.

I called J.J. but I guess he's asleep because I had to just leave a message. I hate that!

July 9th—Wednesday—7:43 p.m.

It was hard telling our students good-bye. They are all pretty much challenges, but they are each individuals, too. I can see why J.J. enjoys teaching so much and finds it so fulfilling. He particularly likes little Bethel. She seems like a wispy waif, and much younger than she actually is. He often patted her little shoulders and rubbed her tiny hands when she was close to tears. Often he even hugged her so tightly that they almost seemed like one. I'm learning so much from him, sometimes I think more than the kids do, because J.J. is such a magnificent, gifted teacher himself. Sometimes I think he could teach crocodiles *to fly* if he really wanted to.

Mrs. Dawson spent the afternoon with us. We had a farewell party for the kids, then she offered to drive me home. I didn't want to go, but J.J. was gushing about how nice it was of her to offer, so I couldn't refuse. Now I wonder how we're going to ever see each other. I hope he's as concerned as I am, but probably he's not. Oh, please, please, J.J., be concerned!

I called his house but had to leave a message because he wasn't home. Where could he be? Now I'm being dumb and foolish and possessive and childish and immature AND ME!

July 10th—Thursday—10:01 a.m.

I called Bridget because I knew she was coming home last night. Nobody answered. This is beginning to seem like the planet of the dead! I wonder where everybody is. Have they all been whisked off into alien space except me? Have I been left here on the decaying, disintegrating earth as a specimen for strange space creatures with their horrible trained half-animals half birds? Whoa! Now I'm making up my own nightmare movie like the one I saw late last night on TV.

10:47 A.M.

Bridget phoned just a minute ago and I was so glad to hear her voice I practically screamed in her ear. She said her whole family had gone to the House of Pancakes for breakfast and she didn't want to wake me up before that although she had zillions of things to tell me.

We yacked for a few minutes, then she said she'd get on her bike and whiz over. She hadn't been on a bike or roller blades or anything else fun since she'd left and she was ready for some wild action! Neither one of our parents like for us to go to the skate park, but we *had to*! And we did!

After we'd locked our bikes and were putting on our roller blades three guys came over and started talking in filthy language about how many bones they had broken and how many lacerations they had, like those things were glorious bravery awards or something. It was disgusting! And when they asked us if we wanted to play Jump Over we were out of there. Nobody was going to come off the curve and jump over *our heads* while we squatted down directly in their path. We dashed away as fast as possible, wearing our roller blades and pushing our bikes.

From there we went to the baby cemetery, and sat on a corner bench and let our brains hang out. It's a quiet, gentle little place with one single tiny circle grave and headstone in the middle of a little grove about as big as a large room. There's a high iron fence around it that's completely covered by ivy, making it absolutely secluded, and anyone can go in. The story is that about eighty or ninety years ago a very wealthy lady had a little baby that died in its sleep and she had the special cemetery built. It's surrounded now by apartment houses, but it's still a quiet, bird-filled secret place that Bridget and I have been to a number of times when we were feeing down. But this time neither one of us is DOWN. She's just waiting breathlessly for tonight, when she can see Brad, and I won't tell her who my boyfriend is even though she begs and begs. I told her I want it to be the biggest surprise of her life. And it will be! Later, when it's time.

Bridget told me about the goods and the bads of tending the three babies and helping her aunt. She loves helping but feels put-upon, too, because she doesn't know any kids there. She started going to church and she loved that and singing in their choir. There are two cute boys and three nice girls there, so if she'd stayed longer she'd probably have hung out with them, but she's happier to be *here* with me and Brad.

Life is funny, isn't it?

9:47 P.M.

I hate to even think this but I'm worried about J.J. It isn't like him not to . . . he knows Mom works and he *could* phone. I was sure I'd have a voice message when I got home. Maybe he was afraid Mom would get it first, but where is he? Could he have stuffed a note in my backpack on the last day of school?

Stupid, stupid me! All the time I've been worrying about J.J., a little scared that something bad might have happened to him or that he had dumped me, this precious little note has been tucked away in my top backpack pocket: "I've been invited to go fishing this weekend with a friend. Don't forget me! Don't forget US! I've been trying to tell you all day but it's been too hectic. Remember when I had you behind the door and Bobby wandered in and nearly caught us?"

Well, at least I'm glad he's got a friend and I've got Bridget.

July 11th—Friday—9:02 p.m.

Bridget and I were together all day long, mostly at her house. It's noisy and frantic over there. Maybe not FRANTIC but action-filled, with all the kids home and her mom puttering about. She cooks and sews and makes crafts. It would be nice to have a mom who's home all the time.

Bridge is sneaking out tonight with Brad, telling her mom she's going to be with me. I don't like that but I'm not the one doing the lying. Though of course I'll have to lie if her mom calls the house. I hate it that she asked me to lie, but I guess I'd expect her to do the same for me if ever I get the chance to go out with J.J.

I wish *he'd* hurry up and get home. Every pore in my body misses him.

Ron called again—it's hard to tell him I can't go out with him, but I know J.J. would *hate* it if I did.

July 13th—Sunday—11:07 p.m.

Mom and I just got in from a weekend at Aunt Meg and Uncle Harry's. We decided to go at the last minute after Bridget's family went camping. It was fun. Aunt Meg wasn't drinking, so she was her real self. We swam in their pool and played doubles in tennis and ate and ate and ate. I had a really, really good time. Families are fun and wonderful. I wish we lived closer to Aunt Meg and Uncle Harry and that she would always be like she was this weekend.

July 14th—Monday—10:42 a.m.

Glorious, glorious Monday! I will never let anyone in my life mention a "blue Monday" again.

I was just sitting here worrying about why J.J. hadn't called when the phone rang and it was HIM!

J.J.! The sound of HIS voice turned the sun to shining and the birds to singing and my heart to racing. He told me how much he'd missed me and how he longed to run his fingers through my hair and stuff. I feel like . . . like I don't know what, but it's wonderful!

I'm meeting him in the alley behind the pharmacy in two hours. Isn't that the most exciting thing that could ever happen? What to wear? How to fix my hair? Will I have time to wash and dry it by then? Oh, happiness and joy! My heart runneth over, whatever that means.

My sweet, sweet, grandma used to say things like that before she had her heart attack. But I can't think about that now; my life is too filled with wonderment, and *I know* she's up in Heaven *looking down on me and smiling*!

5:30 P.M.

This has been the sweetest day of my life. I was with J.J. for four full hours. We drove up to Piney Cove and then walked up a long steep path to a little grotto filled with ferns and beautiful pastel miniature flowers. My left foot was killing me because I'd worn my new sandals, which weren't meant for hiking, but all pain ceased when we sat on a little rock ledge and he hugged me and kissed me and softly rubbed my arms and hands and shoulders. He is so wonderful and tender, and I love him, love him, love him! I was just beginning to feel his heart thumping close to mine when we heard a group of noisy hikers coming toward us. J.J. jumped up and pretended to be showing me the flora and the fauna and explaining them to me.

Later an older man came by with one of his cronies, and looking at us, said with a smile, "I remember when I used to take my little girl out to places like this. Enjoy it while you can, because all too soon she'll be grown up."

I wanted to throw rocks at him or spit in his face or something. How could the nearsighted old coot be so stupid?

After they left, J.J. comforted me and suggested that maybe tomorrow I'd like to come to his house, where, for a change, no one would bother us. He laughed. "We've hardly had time to get to know each other with teachers and janitors and students and now gawkers butting in."

July 15th—Tuesday—4:30 p.m.

I feel like Alice in Wonderland or somebody else not quite real. J.J.'s house is adorable. It's actually a cottage on the back of what used to be a big estate. The main house burned down and they haven't rebuilt it yet. J.J.'s place is so private and away from everything, it's like in another world, and everything in it is so old and comfy that it seems like it's been there since the beginning of time.

At first J.J. seemed a little uncomfortable. He told me almost shyly that he'd been attracted to me like a magnet from the first time he laid eyes on me. He said something about *ME* making *him* feel safe and unafraid and comfortable. Isn't that the most beautiful and amazing thing ever uttered by mankind? He said he'd always been a little untrustful of females in general but that I . . . He stopped and pulled away suddenly like I might hit him or something, then he told me that he'd been hurt a lot by . . . I interrupted him and told him how I'd felt exactly the same way he felt the very first day he came into our class, safe and unafraid.

It has been a fairy-tale kind of day. J.J. showed me around his house like a proud little kid while he talked and talked about his childhood in California. We made out for a little while, then he told me how his parents had divorced when he was young and how his mother had been short-tempered, a screamer and curser. She'd wanted to be an actress and had made him feel like *he* was the reason *she* didn't make it.

I felt soooooo sorry for him my heart about ruptured, and I held him so close and hard my arms ached. No little kid should ever be treated like that!

I asked him if he'd ever thought of running away, and he shrugged and asked, "Run to where?"

No wonder it is hard for him to feel safe and secure around grown-ups! My heart and every pore in my body bleeds for him. I am sooooo grateful he has me! THAT WE HAVE EACH OTHER, because I feel a fraction of what he feels: lonely, left out, insecure, unbelonging, unloved, unlovely . . . UNLOVELY? J.J.? *UNLOVELY?* He's the most lovable, lovely person in the world! Everybody at school adores him! The coach loves him, the janitor, the teachers, the secretaries, the principal, the kids. ESPECIALLY THE KIDS! What's not to love? I think . . . I hope . . . I KNOW! *I* can *help him* regain his self-confidence like he's helped me find mine!

We talked about that for a long, long time, then decided we should change the subject to something happier.

After a few silly suggestions by both of us, J.J. asked seriously, "Jennie, does the difference in our ages bother you at all?"

I reached over and kissed his hand, which he had pulled back from mine. Then I told him in all honest sincerity how much I longed for a mature person in my life to help me find *my* lost, lonely way to wher-ever.

J.J. smiled and told me I really did look like a lost, lonely little kid who needed someone to look after her. He said *he'd* like to look after me. I told him *I'd like* more than anything in the world to *have him* look after me.

We got the giggles then and laughed and laughed until we were both crying. Isn't it funny how you can cry sometimes when it's the happiest time of your life?

Well, anyway, after a minute J.J. looked at me like he was seeing me for the first time. He almost whispered, "Jennie, I see the little child in you. I really do! Let me take your picture *now* so you can see it. So we can have it in our lifetime book of remembrances forever."

I felt strange but sort of wonderful, too, as J.J. excitedly pulled out a big camera and lenses. He said he's always wanted to be a photographer but has never had the time. NOW he has the time *and the model*. I felt like I had died and gone to Heaven. ME a model! Well, it wasn't exactly like I'd expected. He said he wanted me to look as young as possible in these pictures. Later, he said he would photograph me as mature sexy siren. I snickered at that.

"You gotta be kidding," I said. He told me I'd be surprised what he could do.

J.J. cleaned off every bit of blush and lipstick I had on my face and fixed my hair into a sloppy-looking braid on each side with big ribbons. Then he took my shoes off and had me scrunched up in an old blanket with my feet hanging out and flopping over each other.

In one way I was embarrassed; in another way I felt honored. J.J. stepped back and looked so serious it almost scared me, then he smiled and asked me to make a hundred different facial expressions. It took forever and was boring, boring, boring!

I hated it when J.J. took me home but he said he'd pick me up at the same place tomorrow. I said I'd tell Mom I was going to be helping out at the library.

J.J. said he'd have the pictures developed by tonight. I'll be glad because that wasn't my favorite thing in the whole world to do. I hope that part of his project is over.

July 16th—Wednesday—3:30 p.m.

J.J. brought me home early because he had some errands to run. I thought the pictures were dumb, but J.J. *loved them*, so he probably saw something there I didn't see. I guess I'm just looking at the down side as usual or maybe it's the wine cooler. J.J. says a little wine is good for a person but that I should NEVER, NEVER OVERDO IT! And of course I won't. Especially because of his mother's drinking and my Aunt Meg's. He says *they* are like the bad side of a good thing.

July 17th—Thursday—3:32 p.m.

Today J.J. took some pictures of me looking like *I am*, but as young as possible. He had a horrible time getting the exact, precise look he insisted on having on my face, and took so many pictures I almost wanted to scream at him, but of course I didn't. Anyway, I finally looked at him like my mom had met him and said she really liked him and she was glad he was my boyfriend. Then he wanted one more. A look like I was asking him to please make out with me. I smiled, feeling happy but self-conscious as he took a lot of shots and said *that* was exactly what he wanted.

We made out for a little while after that. Then he took me home, saying he wasn't feeling well. I hope it's nothing serious.

9:27 P.M.

I want like everything to call J.J. but he might be asleep. I hope he is! I wonder if there is anything to mental telepathy. I'm going to try it. Maybe he will feel my healing, restful vibrations. Sleep, dear, sweet, most beautiful of all princes . . . relax . . . and heal thyself . . . heal . . . heal thyself . . . and rest.

I hope it's working for him, because it is for me. One more slow, deep breath and I'm ready for la la land.

July 18th—Friday

Today after we'd made out a lot and had had two beautiful crystal long-stemmed glasses of wine together (it tastes just like drinking sweet bubbles) I felt like *I* controlled creation. J.J. told me I was the most gifted, intelligent, beautiful creature in the world. He made me feel like the most precious, desirable, loved, and lovely of all things precious, desirable, and lovely. I was drifting on those wonderful feelings when he whispered in my ear to please take off my blouse and let him take some pictures. I shook my head, then when I saw his sad eyes I felt like I had offended him and smiling shyly I started unbuttoning my shirt.

At that most inappropriate second the phone rang and J.J. smiled and said I had so addled him that he'd forgotten an important appointment.

He had me gargle with Listerine and told me to go home and pop into bed, telling my mom I had cramps or a bad headache when she got home. I didn't have a headache but I did still feel a little fuzzy.

Mom felt sorry for me and made me some milk toast. She's a great mom. Everybody likes and respects her, and she's top gun in her office. I can't understand why, since she has so much common sense, she still thinks I'm a baby. At least she treats me like one and expects me to act like one.

July 19th—Saturday—7:30 p.m.

I'm really shaking in my shoes—actually, all over. Today at work someone gave Mom two tickets to the ballet for working on Saturday. She called the library and I wasn't there, so she thought maybe I was sick or something and called the house. I wasn't there either, so she worried like crazy until two o'clock, when she called again. Thank goodness J.J. had brought me home just before that. It's the first time I've been to his house on a Saturday.

When I answered the phone, I was scared to death because I was still a little bit woozy. J.J. and I had shared some wine during the photography session. He says he's preparing me to be a real model when I'm older, but of course, he says, other photographers *won't* take the pictures he does. He says it's okay if I just do it with him where he can protect me and take care of me if something happens.

I took a long, long, long, long, almost-cold shower to get my brains untangled and the evening was beautiful and fun. I like being with Mom most of the time, and I even don't mind straightening up the house and doing the laundry and dishes when I know that I'm going to J.J.'s afterward.

Sometimes I wonder about the . . . photography stuff . . . but I know J.J. would never do anything, well . . . you know . . . that was wrong.

I have to keep telling myself that we're just playing games and I believe in him and *trust him* implicitly!!!!!

July 26th—Saturday—11:43 a.m.

I've been with J.J. every weekday this week, but weekends are *endlessly* long when I don't see him. I miss him sooooo much it hurts. Yet almost every weekend he has to go out of town to work with problem kids in a juvenile facility. He is so socially conscious and brilliant! He teaches school because he loves it; he teaches those kids because the kids and the people there need him; AND he does photography because he thinks my beauty—my *"untouched beauty and uniqueness"*—should be saved for forever. *He says it so seriously I almost believe him.* I'm so proud of him and flattered that he loves and cherishes me and is teaching me about life and love. Later he's going to teach me about music and art and how my heart and mind and soul work, and everything else that will make me "his clone." I wish!

2:30 P.M.

Time has *stopped* dead in its tracks and I'm bored stiff!!!!!

Mom and I are going biking when she wakes up from her nap. She deserves it. She works too hard but it takes a lot to support a house and me and everything. Three months, October 30, and I'll be fifteen. Maybe then I can get a part-time job that isn't volunteering, so I can help pay at least a part of my way in life, that is—I could if J.J. and I weren't, you know—

2:49 P.M.

I wonder if Mom is ever going to wake up. Maybe she's died. *That's* a horrible thought! And I will never, ever think of it again.

I wonder where Bridget is and what she's doing. I miss her a *lot*! And all the fun, childish, no-worry, no-responsibility, no-brainer times we had when we were little. I miss Marcie and hockey and . . . just being a kid. I wonder if J.J. and I are doing what's right.

THAT'S STUPID! I'm just bored and lonely and friendless, not really friendless because I'll always have J.J., but . . . maybe I don't really want to be grown up.

I just thought of Ron Matterly, Mom's friend's son, the kid I met where we had the Fourth of July celebration. He's not beautiful as a Greek god like J.J., or mature or breathtakingly brilliant, but he was so cool and uncumbered (is that a word?) and simple to be with. Oh, crap! Life is so stupid and complicated and I'm such a lost cause.

2:52 P.M.

I wish I could talk with J.J. like I talked with Ron the very first time we met. I didn't have to be careful or concerned about my grammar or posture or clothes or anything else. I wish . . . oops, I hear Mom getting up. Gotta go. See ya later.

July 27th—Sunday

Duller-than-dull day. Yesterday afternoon was fun. Mom is a good sport, but a kid needs a *kid* friend. J.J. is . . . well, when I'm with him I'm completely overcome and grateful and happy in every way, but . . . forget it! I guess I just want perfection and everything, everything, everything! *NOBODY* GETS *EVERYTHING*, STUPID! FACE IT! WHO DO *YOU* THINK YOU ARE?

July 29th—Tuesday—11:15 a.m.

Haven't written in a few days, but life is going by whirlwind style. I'm lucky because J.J. is helping me straighten things out. He says it's perfectly normal for me to be confused during this changing time in my life, but he almost seemed to resent it when I mentioned Ron and Bridget. I know he thinks they're immature, and I guess he thinks they're holding me back in a childish pattern. I started to tell him *I didn't want* to grow up in one big step but . . . I guess I'm just being paranoid and insecure beyond reality.

When he started talking to me about being together in every way, every day, for forever, I wilted completely and could only think about *US*!

After we'd had some wine and pot J.J. seriously explained to me about the wondrous and intricate details of life and love. He was tender and patient as he made things that had always seemed a little filthy and gross seem beautiful and healthy and God created. We then made out passionately for a little while, and I'm embarrassed to even write this but I really wanted him to go further. I didn't want him to stop, ever, ever! EVER!

He told me he loved me in "a deeply, spiritually committed way" and asked me if I had thought of marriage. When I appeared startled, he said that in some states it was legal for fifteen-year-old girls to marry. Then he asked me, on bended knee, like in an old movie, if I would marry him on my fifteenth birthday, which is October 30th.

At first I actually wanted to run away, then slowly a film of peace seemed to drape over me, *over us*!

After a while J.J. slowly and carefully explained to me that REAL LOVE, to him, was too precious to be taken lightly, that it should *not* be used as most unskilled kids use it, that "LOVEMAKING," he almost whispered, was a holy sacred pleasuring and that when he actually introduced me to it I too would consider it such. Isn't that the most beautiful thing you've ever heard?

How could stringbean, not-all-that-bright *ME* have a Sir Galahad like HIM? But he won't let me talk badly about myself. He says I am as near perfect as someone my age can possibly be and that I will become each day more and more perfect as he molds me. Oh! The thought of having him literally mold me is heavenly. Ummmmmm, I didn't think I would ever consider *heaven* and *sex* in the same way! But J.J. said in the Holy Bible the first commandment given to Adam and Eve in the Garden of Eden was to "multiply and replenish the earth." Then he said with a very serious smile that "God *didn't mean* for them to do it through artificial insemination." Oh, J.J. is so off-this-planet intelligent that he takes my breath away. How fortunate I am to be in his hands, and *of course* he's always right! I wish I could talk to Bridget about some of the nice things that go on between us, because *they* both are so childish and uninformed. But I can't. J.J. doesn't want me to! Isn't that a tragedy?

9:16 P.M.

P.S. I forgot to tell you that J.J. LOVES me more than his very own life. What did I ever do, or *what can* I ever do, to deserve that? He knows *I* would *do anything, be anything,* for HIM! At least I hope he does. He should. I tell him often enough!

I'm so proud of myself that I can keep our secrets!!!!!! I've never before in my life kept a secret.

July 30th—Saturday—9:30 p.m.

It's been a cool, comfy day. I didn't even wake up till after ten this morning. Mom took the car to run a few errands. Run, run as fast as you can. You can't catch me with *my* gingerbread man. Run, run, sun, sun, fun, fun, I won. I won! The prize of all males . . . in all areas. I can hear myself giggling but I'm sort of somewhere else, too. J.J. doesn't know I borrowed a few of his smokes, but I only use them out in the storeroom in my underwear with a shower cap on so Mom can't smell . . . whatever. And now I don't miss Bridget or Marcie or Ron or . . . what's to miss?

The last few days J.J.'s been doing "adult shots" of me. Some of them are beautiful and wispy . . . but others are . . . he calls them "high fashion." He says he wants the pictures so when we're old and gray and fat together we'll remember we were once young and beautiful and . . . you know.

August 2nd—Saturday—9:47 p.m.

I only stay an hour or so every few days at J.J.'s and I'm getting a little ticked off because he won't let me call his house anymore. He says his relatives are coming and going and he doesn't want them to meet me until after we're married. That sounds like crap to me, but then I don't want my mom to meet *him* either until then. I can't wait until we can do all the things together we want to do in front of the whole wide world!

We never go *anywhere* or do *anything*. . . . It's just . . . I don't want to go on this way anymore. I don't know what I'm feeling. The other day, when J.J. gave me some pills to take, I got to feeling sad or neglected or so lonely I wanted to kill myself. I really did. Why would I want to do that? Where has the *REAL*, happy, little-girl *me* gone?

Midnight—exactly

When I looked up at the clock on my dresser and saw what time it was I got soooo mad I wanted to hurt somebody. Imagine *ME*, the sissy, cream puff, protector of all things weak and lowly and lonely in the world, wanting to hurt *all things* weak and lowly and lonely! I really, truly, honestly, for a moment, did! I shivered. Could the weak and lowly, lonely person I wanted to hurt be me?

Scared spitless, I sobbed for a while with my head under the protective covers, then hesitantly dialed J.J.'s number. At first J.J. couldn't even understand me I was so upset, then he slowly and softly told me to put on some clothes and meet him on the corner north of our house.

We drove to "our alley," and he hugged me and kissed me and cried with me and said everything was all his fault. Over and over he blamed himself for giving me too much wine, too much pot, and too many uppers and downers for my size body. "They were meant to be used sparingly and *only* for pleasuring and relaxation!" he said.

After a while I was trying to comfort J.J. as much was he as trying to comfort me. Sweet, sweet, dear, dear J.J. He wouldn't hurt me for anything in the world. EVER! EVER! EVER!!!!

I began begging him to *forgive me*, and he put his head down in my lap and sobbed. My love for him exploded into the whole universe. It was part of the stars and the moon and the velvety soft, protective blackness that tucked us into each other's arms for forever. We were one and always would be. I know! I *really do know* that our love is so great and sacred that it will keep us together "until death do us part." It *WILL NOT* be like my parents' marriage!!!

As J.J. took me back to my house he whispered and sobbed how precious and priceless and beautiful and wonderful and gifted and stuff I was and how much he adored me and didn't mean to ever hurt me.

His loving concern healed me, and as I slipped quietly out of his car at my corner I felt completely restored and renewed. What we are doing *is* right! It is the way it should be and soon we will be married. We haven't decided which state we should go to (one where fifteen-year-olds can marry), but that really doesn't matter. Except that I hope it will be Alaska or southern Georgia or maybe Florida, close to Disney World. Yes, yes, yes! Sunny, funny, fun Florida, next to Disney World!

OR—

Maybe we'll go to one of the wonderfully exciting places J.J.'s told me about like Africa or Egypt or Istanbul or even Azule, Montana, where the deer and the buffalo play. Now I'm being silly.

August 5th

For the last three days J.J. has been too busy to see me or even talk to me on the phone. He's trying to get set up in another school in another state and trying to figure out about our marriage and stuff and actually he's under so much pressure that he sometimes treats me like I'm driving him nuts by being so young and childish and demanding. I'm trying! I really am trying to be mature and like that but I'm as stressed out as he is . . . or maybe not. He's the one with all the responsibilities and I'm doing nothing . . . nothing but worrying myself crazy about us leaving soon and what I'm going to do with all my stuff.

Hmm, maybe I'll go over to his house and take some flowers and homemade cookies and at least get things straightened up. I know he's been too busy to do much of that kind of thing with all of the rest of the stuff that's piling up on him.

I've just been throwing up my guts and my heart. And I'm in some lonely, lost place between Never Never Land and *Never Was Land*! It's so sad and broken here that I'm losing, or maybe have already lost, my mind. I want to die. I want to just shrivel up and become part of all the black ugly nothingness that blocks out pain so deep it's literally rotting every single corpuscle in my soul, whatever a soul is.

I can't believe I was once happy. Happy and prancing up the cobblestone path to J.J.'s house wrapped in warmth and belonging. I'd seen him take the house key out from under the big geranium pot and so I did it and entered the house. It was in utter confusion. Obviously he was in the middle of moving. I didn't know where to start. So I started in the kitchen. There were scrambled eggs spilled on the stove and leftover food on the table. I scrubbed and cleaned it, which helped me feel needed and wanted until the phone rang. The answering machine was on, and my heart stopped beating in its tracks when a guy's voice said, "Yo, bro, it's Bruce, and I hear this time you've got yourself in a screw-up that's gonna be hard to get out of."

I sank into a chair shaking with fear that something bad had happened to J.J. until the unbodied voice said something like, "I thought you'd learned your lesson about getting involved with chickie littles"—a loud long snicker—"but I'll *still* help you get a job in California. They're scrambling to hire subs here. And you can sleep on my couch till you find a dig and *YOU'RE RIGHT*! YOU *GOTTA* DUMP THAT JAIL-JELL and *NOW*! Bring all the yummy pictures you took and start runnin' as soon and as fast as you can *before* she *talks* to someone—and you are really in deep shit."

It's funny how my body kept moving even after my mind shut down completely. I was like a zombie on the bus ride home. Even now I'm like truly, really insane, crazy, deranged, psychotic. Will it last forever? Was J.J. a horrible hallucination? Is he real? What did the phone voice mean about J.J.'s being involved with other "chickie babies" or "chickie littles" or whatever? And *why* was he thinking of running away without me? Didn't he *ever* really like me . . . or love me . . . or anything?

How could he for such a long time have acted like he did and told me how beautiful and wonderful and gifted and stuff I was and how he wanted to take care of me for the rest of my life?

Take care of me? Tears streamed down my face and stained and drained my soul. All I could think of was wanting to jump off the bus into the middle of the traffic and be dead.

It's late and dark and scary and I'm crumpled up in bed. I don't even recognize my handwriting. I feel like I'm completely brain-dead, well, almost completely brain-dead. I've heard that some people have brain damage because of drug and alcohol use, but I haven't used that much, or do some brains have brain drain with very little use?

COME ON! GET REAL, LITTLE SNOT-NOSED KID! You heard with your own ears that old master J.J. was trying to get rid of you.

I feel like I'm being tortured, with my heart literally gouged out of a huge gash J.J. made in my pathetic, repulsive little nothing chest.

I hate. . . (I won't even write his name) more than I knew it was possible to hate! I want to claw out his eyes and puncture his black, evil, kid-hurting heart. How could he do this to a kid like me? To anybody?

I wish I knew more about God and Jesus. They're supposed to help people at times like this. Or are they? Do they even care about people like me?

The very scariest thing about this whole mess is that Jonathan Johnstone is not a made-up person in a book or a movie like Dr. Jekyll and Mr. Hyde. HE'S REAL! And I'm caught in his sticky, evil, obscene web, and I'll never, through my life, be able to get out of it. Oh, please, please, God, let me die. I feel so guilty! So dirty, so used!!!

Mom came home and sat on the side of my bed and comforted me while I cried through the long scary night. She asked me "What's wrong, baby?" but I couldn't answer. I guess I went to sleep. When I woke up she was curled beside me and I was clutching her until I'm sure I've left scratches on her back and shoulders.

Never did she try to force me to answer her questions or tell me to grow up or anything like I expected her to. She just, Mom-like, rubbed her sweet-smelling, soft hands across my forehead and whispered, "It's okay, Jennie. It's going to be okay. You'll see. We got through one catastrophe, we can get through this one, whatever it is, too. We can do it, Jennie. Together we can do it!" Slowly she cooed over and over, with her tears joining mine. "We *can* do it. We *can* do it." Almost subconsciously I started saying it with her: "We can do it. We can do it. We *can* do it."

All day I've stayed in bed, almost lifeless, getting up only to go to the bathroom. It's like I'm floating somewhere between reality and unreality in nothingness. Mom puts the phone on my bedside before she left so I could call her if I need to or she can check on me. When she's around, I pretend that I just have an upset stomach and diarrhea from something I've eaten.

When Mom got home, I could hardly raise my head off the pillow and I'd wet the bed. I was *sooooo* humiliated. I hadn't done that since I was a little teeny, tiny kid. I wondered what was happening to me and clung to Mom like I was drowning and scared witless.

She held me so tightly in her arms we were almost like one. After a long time she said gently, "Talk to me,

Jennie, please talk to me. Honestly, most often talking helps more than anything."

I tried again, but I couldn't! I really couldn't! I'd die before I'd ever let my dear mom know the horrible, unbelievable things I'd done. I felt like a leper who had just come out of the sewers covered from my head to my feet with . . . you know . . . stinking and unforgivable and unworthy. OH, SO UNWORTHY OF ANYTHING, *EVER*, THAT WAS FOR GOOD PEOPLE.

Mom looked deeply into my eyes, and she must have seen every bit of the evil crud that was swiftly dissolving my mind and my body and my soul because she started sobbing in a tortured animal sort of way. I thought *she must know* what I couldn't possibly talk about. I shivered. How would she know?

After what seemed like ages and ages of quiet suffering for both of us she started whispering in a voice so low I had to strain to hear her, "Baby, I *don't know* what's eating at you but *I love you*. You know that. You are my life, the one thing that makes my existence joyful and worthwhile. You're part of my heart."

I put my hands tightly over my ears but I couldn't keep the words or the pain out. She kept talking and talking. It was like she couldn't stop and I couldn't die like I wanted. She'd probably want to dump me, too, if she really knew. So I wouldn't tell her. I wouldn't! I couldn't!

Finally when we were both completely exhausted she kept saying over and over, "It's okay, baby. It really is okay and *you're* going to be all right. I understand your pain. I really do understand!"

But that was the problem. SHE DIDN'T! SHE

COULDN'T! The difference between her and me was . . . she could be forgiven for anything she'd done by that great Someone God in that great Somewhere Place . . . but me . . . I began shaking like I was having a seizure of some kind and my teeth were clacking together so loudly they chomped at my brain and I couldn't stop them.

Mom wrapped herself around me so tightly I felt at last safe and protected, and suddenly, though I tried to keep them back, the words began sputtering and drooling and popping out of me completely out of my control. I could hear the ugliness and the evil crawling out like millions of poisonous slithering nonthings, but Mom wouldn't let them kill us. She started praying to God to help us and I started praying with her. I'd never heard my Mom pray before and I'd never prayed myself. Surprisingly, it seemed to push out a lot of the heavy depraved blackness that seemed about to overtake us.

It was after midnight by the time Mom had pulled me together and we went into the kitchen to get some dinner.

After we sat in silence for a few minutes, I reached over and touched Mom's hand sympathetically because I could see the pain in her all over.

She took both of my hands and squeezed them tightly. "We can't let *your* offender get away with it, Jennie. We *can't*! We'd never be able to forgive ourselves if we let him do to others what he has done to you."

I hung my head. NO MATTER WHAT, I WOULD *NEVER* LET MOM KNOW ALL THE GORY DETAILS OF WHAT HAD REALLY HAPPENED TO ME! I *COULDN'T*! I *WOULDN'T*!

Mom seemed to be reading my mind. "Truly, Jennie, you would always feel guilty if you don't do something to keep . . ." Her eyes opened wide. "Jennie, was it . . ."

I covered my ears and started crying loudly, "NO, NO, NO, NO, NO!"

Mom mouthed, without speaking, "Mr. Johnstone?"

His name thundered through my brain. How could she have known? I wouldn't hurt him! I couldn't hurt him! I loved him and he loved me. We were going to get married. I was probably drunk and stoned and the things I thought had happened hadn't really happened at all! He was the best thing that had ever come into my life. He made me feel precious! And wanted! And adored! And important! I would not accuse him! No one could make me! How could I destroy him when he had done so much for me? Had made me so happy and self-confident and secure?

Mom put her soft hand on my forehead. "Go back to bed and sleep on it," she said lovingly. "I know it's a monstrous decision for a young person like you." She gulped. "And it won't be easy."

I watched two big tears zigzag down her face but I still couldn't say yes.

After a long time of trying to go back to sleep, I got up and crawled into bed with Mom. It was obvious she hadn't been able to sleep either. She told me again how much she loved me, how much she had always loved me, and that she would love me forever, no matter what I decided to do or not to do.

For a minute I was torn, then I could hear the guy on the phone telling horrible J.J. to get away fast and *bring the pictures with him*! Pictures that were to be my and J.J.'s secret. I couldn't believe it! We'd promised! They would be just for us!

Stupid, gullible me! I pulled away from Mom. I didn't want to get any of filthy *me* on her.

More tears than I thought were left in me began to flow, and I whimpered, "How did you know? How could you tell?"

I hardly recognized her voice when she started telling me that she had become the slightest bit suspicious when I began talking about Mr. Johnstone like he was perfect and could do no wrong. In a cold monotone she told me how she had stayed awake berating herself for the bad thoughts she had about Mr. Johnstone and had finally convinced herself that she was just being paranoid. After a while she said she thought I needed to go to a rape center to talk things out and find closure. Just as *she* needed to seek help for her pill problem.

I couldn't stop myself then and told her about the little-girl pictures.

She didn't cry or get mad or anything. She just said over and over, "Jennie, we can't let that degenerate get away with what he's done to you—and probably girls before you—and go on to do the same or worse to other little girls and possibly boys, can we? Please say we can't, Jennie, because in some way then WE would be partially responsible, wouldn't we?"

For a minute she seemed like she was the child and I was the mother. "Wouldn't we, Jennie?"

I gritted my teeth and ground out the words, "But he didn't rape me, Mom." I took a deep breath. It's hard to tell things like this to your mom. "He really didn't. I was the one that . . . that . . . wanted to do it."

"But he set you up for it, didn't he?"

"Yeah . . . I guess," I said, not knowing where to turn.

Mom looked at me pleadingly. "Would you care if I called the rape center and we just went down to talk?"

I wanted to say no but my mouth said, "Okay."

I can't believe how fast things are going. Mom called the rape center and we were told to come down immediately. A nice older lady took down some simple information and then we went in to talk to a younger lady named Laurel. She had big pictures of her kids and her dogs and her husband around the room. She shook my hand solemnly and then smiled like the sun had come out from behind a cloud. "You may not think you're going to live through this, kiddo, but you are, believe me, you are."

Something in her eyes, for a second, said she'd been . . . you know . . . too, but she didn't actually say it.

Mom told her we'd like to put Mr. Johnstone in prison, and I shivered because even then I *didn't want to* almost more than I did want to.

Mom went out of the room to talk to someone else, and forever Laurel and I talked about rape. Well, mainly she talked. I was amazed how she knew absolutely—well, almost absolutely—everything about Mr. Johnstone. About his saying such wonderful things to me and about me, and how he'd at first just stroked my hair and rubbed my shoulders and . . . it was almost like a paint-by-the-numbers picture. As she talked, I began to feel more and more used and less and less responsible. But I still felt that he was an ax murderer and he was still hacking away at me, and

I would always and forever have scars that people could see for miles.

Laurel told me that predators often use on their victims the same tactics that he (his name tastes like throw-up when I use it) used. But that didn't heal my anguish much, especially when she started talking about what would happen if we filed charges against him.

Later, Laurel and Mom and I talked for a long time. Actually, Laurel talked about how Mr. Johnstone would probably deny everything. I couldn't believe that at first, but I couldn't disbelieve it either after what I'd heard on the phone. Of course, I hadn't told them about the phone call or the really bad pictures, but some Jell-O shaky stuff inside me was giving me hints that I might have to. But I won't! That would hurt my mom too much and make her so ashamed of me that in her eyes I'd always be an unforgivable slut, scumbucket, thrown-up hairball.

We went over to talk to a police person and I closed up like a clam. He looked a lot like Mr. Johnstone, young and beautiful and friendly. I couldn't, I *wouldn't,* trust him, but my mouth wouldn't open up to tell him so. I wanted to shout at him that he was probably one of them too, but nothing would come out of me but tears and sharp mutilating pain.

Officer Whatever and Laurel tried to talk to me for a long time before I found myself able to ignore *him* and talk to her.

I feel some better about myself, but of course I haven't told her or anybody the worst stuff. Everybody has great sympathy and compassion and understanding for me, especially Laurel. I almost know for sure she'd been through the whole disgusting thing.

I have a new older policeman I'm going to talk to.

I hope he doesn't remind me of J.J.! How can bad "predators" seem so good?

Mom's been with me every step and I'm glad, but I'm not glad, too, because I don't want her to have to relive my body horrors and mind horrors. I'm appreciative, though, in the very most inner part of me, that she insists on going! She's a good mom. The very kind I want to be when I grow up.

Everything everybody said in the police station sounded scary and sometimes even threatening, but I am beginning to feel like Mom does—that we *have* to go through with it to save other kids, some probably even lots younger than me.

10–SOMETHING P.M.

I couldn't believe it when I opened our front door and Dad was there. I didn't know whether to hug him or spit on him and hit him. Then I saw the tears streaming down his face and I thought I'd die from his pain as well as mine, right there on the porch.

I guess we must have said something or made some kind of noise, because Mom came running and pulled us both into the house.

It was a weird reunion with all of us crying and wiping our noses and faces on anything that was handy. Mom and Dad were both apologizing all over each other and I was feeling like a Ping-Pong ball in the middle. Mom held my hand so tight I felt like every bone was being smashed to smithereens but I liked it too because it made me feel safe and proved she WOULD NOT LET GO OF ME EVER! I needed that.

After a little while I tuned in on what they were trying to say to each other and I heard Mom telling Dad she had been wrong, wrong, wrong in telling him I didn't want to see him when she was actually the one, and that she'd torn up his letters so I wouldn't see them, and the one I'd written to him, too, and changed our phone number to a private one . . . I thought because she had to . . . but she said it was because she didn't think he deserved to talk to me. I was so shocked I couldn't speak, and I felt more guilty and dirty and horrible than ever that *I had caused* them to do such awful things to each other.

After a little the atmosphere softened and we found ourselves hugging in a tight little circle. Trying to stay afloat singly and together. It seemed they felt like I did that we were all we had! It was pathetic in a way, but healing, too.

Dad thanked Mom every which way for allowing him to be a part of the court case and for accepting his monthly check on the house payment. I didn't know that, and for one instant I felt used and abused by both of them till I realized how severely they both were hurting. Selfish, self-centered ME who had brought all the problems upon myself wasn't the only one who was suffering physically and mentally because of my stupidity.

Three days later—whatever this day is

Dad says he'll take off all the time that's needed to help. Everything is so hurried and dirty and messy and

I'm so confused and mad at myself for getting everyone into this mess. But it's nice, too, having Dad staying with us even if he sleeps in the little guest room . . . MAYBE . . . but my mind can't think of anything but *my* advocate pretending over and over that *he's* J.J. or *his attorney.* (J.J.'s not even a person to me anymore; he's a monster eating-*me* creature that tries to dismember and devour me in my nightmares, both physically and mentally.)

I don't know if J.J.'s in jail or out on bail or what. I do hope he's not in jail! I've heard such horrible stories on *20/20* and other shows about what happens to handsome sweet guys like J.J. in jail. I hate his guts but . . . Mom and Laurel and Dad all say that *IN THIS ONE CASE* IN MY LIFE I HAVE TO *CONCENTRATE ON THE BAD* INSTEAD OF THE GOOD! It's hard . . . but it's good too. I don't want any other girl in the world to be hurt and scared like I've been. Will I ever trust again? Ever love? Ever have confidence? Ever be the least bit secure and happy? Everybody keeps telling me I will . . . but . . . I don't know. I don't think so!

I still haven't told anyone about the real bad stuff. That would truly make my parents hate me and despise and be disgusted by me forever! But it really truly wasn't all my fault completely. He got me thinking he was so perfect and holy that I should almost worship him. In a way I think I did! But nobody would believe that.

This thing is going on forever. I can't understand how each minute I become more exhausted and not-me anymore and lifeless. How everything in life has become totally gray and sort of green Jell-O-ish. I feel like an old, old, beaten, crippled, gray, gray, senile, barely-able-to-navigate ghost of a beaten-up, worn-out carcass.

Terrible Mr. Johnstone looks right through me, like I'm not even there. That's the worst! Maybe I am a nobody nonperson who doesn't deserve to be on the earth. He's winning! Everybody believes him! Not me! I know it!

Another eon. I think I've gone crazy. Last night I dreamed about the time J.J. asked me to have lunch with him in the park on Saturday, after I told my mom I was going to play baseball. I was so elated that I remember thinking I was running two feet off the ground as I tried to find the hidden sheltered little lost green grotto he'd told me about and how my heart sang, especially after J.J. (he was still *MR.* Johnstone then) gave me a darling little necklace with one tiny music note on it. We talked for three hours, and he pried out of me my complete life story. I can even now almost feel his tender hug as he told me he felt like I was the daughter anyone, including him, would be privileged and honored to have. Then he again asked me to become his assistant in grading math papers. Did that really happen? And if it did, how and when did he turn into the horrible monster I am now trying to send to jail? Maybe I was hallucinating then and am hallucinating now! BUT I'M NOT!

Time has stopped. At last it is over, and nothing has leaked out in the papers or on TV with my picture saying what a trash garbage dump tramp I am. The whole thing is kind of fuzzy, not real anymore. I remember Mr. Johnstone seeming to be the good guy and *me* the predator. He told everyone how I chased him and how he'd loved me as a student and tried to do everything in his power to make me feel better about my *poor little insecure, inadequate self.* Tears came to his eyes as he whimpered about how devastated he felt that I was trying to take away his teaching certificate, as well as ruin his reputation, and he couldn't imagine why.

I suddenly had my belly full of his crappy lies and stuff and whispered to Mom about my diary and *his* notes. Mom whispered to Laurel and she had the case recessed for an hour and a half while we went home to get my treasure box.

When the judge saw the notes and the necklace, which they traced to the jeweler, J.J. was dead meat. AND I'M GLAD!!!! But I'm not glad, too—crazy, mixed-up me.

At least they told me I won't have to come back here again—EVER!!!

I got up to go to the bathroom and Mom and Dad were on the couch. They were sitting close and whispering so I sneaked back into my room. What if? I can't wait to go to sleep and dream about the possibilities. Is everything really over and can we all three possibly LIVE HAPPILY EVER AFTER?

Sweet, sweet dreams

Come to me soon

And take me to

The stars and moon.

Away from all the stuff that's bad

Into a world

That's good and glad.

My wish wasn't to be. Dad is leaving today for his home in Seattle AND HIS NEW WIFE. He's made me promise I'll come stay with them during my Christmas vacation but I *won't* leave Mom for long! She only has me. Not much! But I guess I'm maybe better than nothing!

September 16th

Mom and I just got back from taking Dad to the airport for the last trip here. She and I are both going to go see Laurel for counseling at the rape crisis center. We both need to get our lives recentered. I never realized till today, when we talked, just how fearful of life Mom has always been. She's certainly put on a good front all these years.

September 28th

I've decided I'm too old for a diary, but I'm certainly glad I kept one during the time of . . . oops . . . I'm trying to push that part of my life so far away from me that it will be like nothing, a vague, barely there nightmare of the past. I've got to admit, though, that my diary and J.J.'s notes (I'd kept them and the necklace even though he'd told me not to) *won our case hands down*, and that rotten old viper J.J. is going to jail and his teaching license is being revoked. When they searched his house they found many copies of our pictures, and when they checked his past they found at least one other girl whose mother wouldn't let her prosecute him. In fact, when Principal Doney had told J.J. it wasn't prudent for him to have me as an aide, it was because there was some question on his records. Mr. Doney *never even bothered* to take the time to find out more! I am so humiliated! How could I *not* have seen him for what he really is?

Oh, that reminds me, Mom and I started going to church. She said when she was young she was really close to God and Jesus. Now she's teaching me to be close to them, too, *so they can be close to me!* It's a wonderful and safe and sane feeling, and I'm happy as a clam, however happy that is. Oh, and the Bridget-Brad thing is totally over, dead and buried. He's cheated on her for the *last* time! *We're* again Siamese sisters zipped at the hip. Isn't that the greatest! Maybe someday I'll tell her *everything* about J.J. and . . . you know. But probably not!

October 13th

For my birthday, October 30th, Mom's giving me a party at the Ice Palace, which has recently reopened. LIFE IS BEGINNING TO BE, AT LEAST SOMETIMES, GLORIOUSLY GLORIOUS AGAIN! What else can I tell you?

October 30th

In the middle of the night a horrible nightmare woke me up. My blood was freezing and my skin crawling, and I had to sneak into Mom's room. Feeling unworthy to be too close to her, I wrapped the blanket I had been pulling along behind me into a cocoon and curled up by the door. How could I ever have let *him* touch me? I felt like . . . my skin was falling off in huge gory patches down to the bone.

After a while Mom woke up and coaxed me into her bed. There we talked about when I was a little baby and when Bridget and I were in grade school, and how someday the three of us, Bridget, Marcie, and me, would go to college together. After a bit we reassured each other, over and over, that IT HADN'T BEEN *OUR* FAULT when the bad thing happened in our lives. Hers the divorce and mine . . . you know. Laurel said we should do that again and again until we finally with all our hearts *believed it*! She said the believing part was hard for many rape victims! She says I *really was raped*, or at least victimized, which is the same thing.

November 2nd

I'm back in my own safe snugly white bed, with my safe snugly stuffed baby bunny asking myself over and over IF A PART OF ME WILL *ALWAYS BE BROKEN*! Nothing happened for what seemed a long time and maybe I dropped off to sleep. I thought I saw a light. It was soft yet bright, and I *felt* more than heard the words "*ONLY* IF *YOU LET IT*."

Was I dreaming? I can't wait to talk to Mom and Bridget about it! Maybe even Ron Matterly. He came to my Ice Palace party, and he's as comfortable as an old shoe, whatever that means. He'd be nice to talk to.

Oh how I wish

That in my dark and dismal

Long ago

Before the bad things got their start

I'd listened

To the sweet still voice

That whispered

Deep within my heart.

Questions and Answers

. . .

Q. Are there a lot of teachers and coaches and other
people at schools that try to seduce kids?

A. *Not many, but enough so that all students should be
aware that there are predators around and that most of
them are very skillful in manipulating both kids and
adults!*

. . .

Q. How can I tell if someone is trying to seduce me?

A. *We all like to hear compliments and have people tell us
how good and great and wonderful we are. Sometimes
predators simply commiserate (show sorrow or
understanding, sympathize and pretend to care) and
sometimes really care so much that they allow their
emotions to rule their actions! It is sad that kids must
be ever aware that sometimes verbalizations and
actions are simply tricks to get them into a web.*

. . .

Q. How can I tell when a teacher is just being nice and
caring and when they are . . . you know.

A. *Unless you are a very shy, lonely, or low-esteemed
person, you should have intuitions that warn you when
someone is becoming too physical or intimate. If you
suspect something isn't right, talk to someone. If you
can't talk to your parents, find a friend or an adult you
feel comfortable talking to about your situation. As a
last resort, talk to yourself. You'll be surprised at how*

much common sense and good judgment you have!

· · ·

Q. **What should I do if I decide someone is trying to hit on me?**

A. *Don't be afraid to report that person to a counselor, the principal, your parents, or the police. If you can't bring yourself to do that, write an anonymous note to one or more of the above. You will not only be helping yourself, you may be helping other innocent young people because predators, if not apprehended, continue their conquests.*

· · ·

Q. **What are some of the things I should watch out for?**

A. *1. Someone touching you inappropriately.*
2. An adult wanting to spend time alone with you when that time is not school-oriented.
3. When an adult offers you drugs, alcohol, or any kind of pornographic material.
4. When someone wants you to keep your relationship (sports, school, church, etc.) a secret.

· · ·

Crisis Lines

. . .

Q. Where can I turn if something happens to me?

A. *You can call any crisis line in your local telephone book or you can call any of the following free numbers:*

. . .

Sexual Assault Crisis Line • • • • • 1-800-643-6250
Boys Town (which also includes girls now) • • 1-800-448-3000
Hope LIne • • • • • • • • • • • • • 1-800-656-4673
National Youth Crisis Hot Line • • • • 1-800-448-4663

. . .

Any of these numbers will have sensitive, knowledgeable people who can help you better understand and find solutions to your problems. Just talking to a stranger sometimes helps sort things out and lessens the stress so you can go on to talk to others.

Also, many schools have student hot lines where anyone can anonymously report serious situations that need to be addressed.

. . .

Q. If I called any of these crisis lines, would they want to know my name or other personal information?

A. *Absolutely not! These calls are completely confidential and you will give only information you feel comfortable giving.*

. . .

Gripping, true-life accounts
for today's teens
Edited by
Beatrice Sparks, Ph.D.

IT HAPPENED TO NANCY
She thought she'd found love…
but instead lost her life to AIDS.

ALMOST LOST
The True Story
of an Anonymous Teenager's
Life on the Streets

ANNIE'S BABY
The Diary of Anonymous,
A Pregnant Teenager

Available wherever books are sold.